THE MONTH
BEFORE
CHRISTMAS

THE MONTH
BEFORE
CHRISTMAS

PAT SCHUCH

Integra Resources LLC
Brighton, Michigan 48116

THE MONTH BEFORE CHRISTMAS

Library of Congress Cataloging-in-Publication Data

Schuch, Pat.
The month before Christmas / Pat Schuch.
1. Christian   2. Inspiration   3. Romance
4. Christmas

1st Edition
ISBN-13: 978-1-942846-67-3 (paperback)

Front Cover Design by Emily Rennich
Back Cover Photo by Patrick Rennich
Back Cover Silhouette Design by Emily Rennich

Published by:
Integra Resources LLC
Brighton, MI 48116
In cooperation with Primedia eLaunch LLC

DEDICATION

This book is dedicated to my special 19-year-old granddaughters, Kristen Grace and Emily Joy (EmJ), whose age, character, determination, spirit, and intelligence, inspired me to write Ruth's story.

SPECIAL THANKS

I want to express my thanks to my husband Jon—my constant companion, supporter, and witness to my many adventures in adulthood.

My heartfelt gratitude also goes out to our daughter Jean Schuch Rennich, whose talent, skills, and attention to detail have been invaluable in the editing of this book.

Deepest appreciation must be expressed to those special friends and relatives who did early readings and provided feedback to improve this book. May God bless you abundantly for generously donating your time and talent to support this project.

This Christmas novella is based on a true story.

All names and many details have been changed.

CONTENTS

PART I

> "Therefore encourage one another
> and build one another up,
> just as you are doing."
> ~ 1 Thessalonians 5:11

Turning 50

Sunday, November 21, 1999, 3:00 pm

I can't believe I'm about to turn fifty. In one month, I'm going to officially start to be old—how depressing.

When Ruth Tanner first became a grandma, she was too excited to feel old. But now with grandchild number three on the way, plus the realization of an upcoming milestone birthday, her usual daily glance at the full-length mirror in her closet became extended.

She noted with a grimace the extra 30 pounds on her 5'3" frame that detracted from her overall appearance, as well as her lower abdomen scarred from two emergency C-sections and a hysterectomy. Fortunately her face was relatively wrinkle-free with only a hint of crow's feet around her brown eyes, and some faint lines on her forehead.

Her hair, once naturally dark brown, but now increasingly gray, was kept youthful by regular dye jobs. Nevertheless, aging seemed to be having an adverse effect on her career. It had been years since she had been promoted, and it was a well-known unwritten rule in her company that if you didn't make it to an executive position by the age of 50, it just wasn't going to happen.

Stepping away from the mirror feeling discouraged, Ruth called her mom and asked if she had experienced similar emotions when she hit the half-century mark.

The 72-year-old explained, "Heavens no, Ruth. At that time we were still parenting two kids—Charlie was 12 and Stan was 17—and your father and I were too busy trying to make ends meet to even think about getting old."

"Oh yeah," said Ruth, recalling how amazing it was that her parents somehow raised six kids, who each went to college, all on her dad's modest tool maker's wages. "I forgot that at 50, even though you had two grandkids just like I do now, your duties at home with the boys kept you feeling young."

"Well," shared her mom, "my 60th was the difficult decade birthday for me. That's when I started having issues with arthritis and other ailments that gave me a newfound respect for aging. Now, when I feel old, all I can do is be grateful to God for all that I can still do and all that He has given me—and try to enjoy life. Take it from me, 50 is not old—50 is young!"

Ruth ended the call thanking her mom for the pep talk. Heeding the sage advice, her positive inner voice reminded her, *I have so much to feel grateful for—my good health, a loving hard-working husband, two adult children married with jobs they enjoy, a supportive extended family within driving distance, wonderful neighbors and friends, and a challenging career. So, why do I have this bad case of the birthday blues?*

Suddenly an idea floated into Ruth's mind

that displaced her depressing thoughts. She wasn't sure if the notion was something she had read about a while ago, something she had just invented, or something that God was inspiring her to do. She thought, *Everyone keeps in touch with special family members and friends who are a regular source of inspiration and influence. But what about those few important individuals, who enter into our lives only briefly and yet change us forever. Wouldn't they be happy to find out how they had significantly impacted someone's life for the better? I know I would.*

After some reflection, two names came to mind. The first was Sister Mary Beatrice, the high school physics teacher who, in 1967, had inspired Ruth to become an engineer. The second was Karl Mensch, a college student she had dated in 1969, who taught her about cultural differences, love, and how to think outside the box. Expressing gratitude to these two people from her past felt like a meaningful way to celebrate her 50th birthday, and distract her from the gloom she was feeling about aging. Locating Karl before her December 22nd birthday seemed unlikely since the last she knew he lived in Germany, but finding Sister Beatrice certainly should be doable—if she was still alive.

With renewed energy and excitement, Ruth pulled out her personal journal, which her grandmother had given to her when she turned 16. Grandma Sophie had emigrated from Poland to America and although she was poor, she wore a fine pearl necklace for important religious holidays like Easter and Christmas. As a young girl, Ruth was always mesmerized by Grandma Sophie's pearl necklace, so it was only fitting that the journal had a string of pearls on the cover. Ruth decided to use the special journal sparingly, to record only precious pearls of wisdom she discovered as she lived her life, in honor of her grandmother.

1. Express gratitude regularly for all the good people and things in your life.

2. Think about doing something special for someone else, if you want to chase away the blues.

High School

1967

Some people believed that attending a girls' high school in Indianapolis like Divine Mercy in the 1960's had to be stifling—strict rules, few extra-curricular activities, and no boys. For Ruth, the opposite was true. She felt privileged to attend a good school with a strong academic focus, appreciating how her frugal parents sacrificed to make the tuition payments. She loved delving deeply into subjects of every kind—science, math, music, drama, philosophy, religion, art, languages, and literature. The only subject that confounded her was gym class, and the two B+ grades she got in physical education were enough to knock her out of the coveted class valedictorian and salutatorian slots into the third place rank in her class of 293.

Ruth liked wearing a school uniform, because it saved time not having to decide what to wear to school each day, and it put her on a more equal footing with the rich girls who attended her school. Her mom always said, "It doesn't matter what clothes you wear or how your hair looks. If you're wearing a smile, people won't notice anything else."

Ruth enjoyed the girls who were her class-mates and appreciated not having the distraction of boys in class. She liked being around boys—just not all the time, and not when she was studying. Through various activities outside of school, there were plenty of boys to interact with from two local boys' high schools and three nearby public high schools.

In her junior and senior years, she had managed to secure roles in the prestigious musical productions put on by the nearest boys' high school. She was an officer in her church's youth group, participated in a community Junior Achievement organization, and worked part time at a nearby drug store's soda fountain. Through these activities, Ruth dated and formed a number of friendships with boys from a variety of schools. The time she spent with them was not so much for romance, but to explore their minds in long conversations on a variety of topics. One of her male friends laughingly told Ruth she was a philomath, but refused to tell her what that meant. When she looked up the word, it was defined as 'a person who loves learning for the sake of learning'—a fairly accurate description of herself, she had to admit.

~~~~~

At Divine Mercy High School, a petite and very energetic teacher named Sister Beatrice walked quickly down the halls, like a human dynamo. On some days, to complement her traditional nun's habit, she wore a tool holster on her belt next to her rosary. Equipped with two screwdrivers, a hammer, and pliers, Sister Beatrice was ready to make repairs in the high school facility that were too challenging for the school's maintenance man, whose primary specialty was mopping floors.

To her students, Sister Beatrice was a jack-of-all-trades who could fix anything. Stories about her were legendary. One day the algebra teacher ran into Ruth's physics classroom exclaiming, "Father Andrew just finished celebrating the Freshmen Mass in the chapel and discovered his car has a flat tire. He doesn't know how to change it and is going to be late for his meeting with the Bishop!" Sister Beatrice ran out of the room, and the whole class watched out the second floor classroom window. The petite sister unloaded the spare tire, took out the jack, and proceeded to change the tire in less than 15 minutes.

Sister Beatrice's passion for all aspects of physics—including statics, dynamics, optics, electricity, and relativity—was contagious. Ruth was like a sponge in class, absorbing every bit of knowledge possible from the feisty teacher, and thoroughly enjoying all the associated lab work. Unlike the biology and chemistry classes Ruth had found interesting, physics was so exciting to her, and she lost track of time while doing the work. She wanted to be just like Sister Beatrice—energetic, smart, caring, and able to solve problems and fix anything that was broken.

One day, sensing that Ruth had been distracted during class, Sister Beatrice stopped her later to ask if everything was okay. Ruth apologized, then confessed that there was one question on the math section of the SAT that she couldn't answer, and being unable to solve it was driving her crazy. She then told the nun the specifics of the problem she remembered so vividly from the standardized test:

A cylinder has a height of 10 inches and a circumference of 4 inches. A string is wrapped one time around the cylinder starting at point A on the top and ending at point B on the bottom directly below point A. How long is the string?

Ruth figured that if you ran a string directly from point A to point B, the answer would be the height of 10 inches. She also reasoned that if you wrapped the string around the circumference from point A back to point A, and then down to point B, the answer would be the circumference of 4 inches plus the height of 10 inches, which equaled 14 inches. The problem stated that the string wrapped around the cylinder one time from top to bottom seemingly in a spiral, so she reasoned that the solution had to be between 10 inches and 14 inches. However, Ruth was stuck on how to proceed to get the exact answer.

Sister Beatrice's advice to Ruth was this: "If you can't solve a problem, write out what you know and draw a sketch." Ruth thanked her for the advice, and smiled since the sister always said that about physics problems. When she got home from school that day, still baffled by the problem, Ruth decided to write to one of her smart friends at an out-of-state college for help since her math teachers had not provided a solution. In the process of writing out and drawing the problem in the letter, the solution came to her.

Visualizing the cylinder as a soup can with a label that had been removed and laid flat as a rectangle, the string wrapped around the cylinder followed the same path as a diagonal line on the can's label. Using the Pythagorean Theorem for triangles ($a^2 + b^2 = c^2$), familiar to every seventh grader, the answer was the square root of $10^2 + 4^2$, that is the square root of 116, which is 10.77 inches.

Ruth was overjoyed at solving the problem and the first person she told was Sister Beatrice, whose drawing method had worked. Decades later, Ruth still remembered that particular SAT problem because of the difficulty she had experienced in solving it.

1. Cultivate platonic friendships with men and women of all ages, as they can be very rewarding.

2. Draw or put a problem down on paper, when you are trying to solve it. That can often help you to visualize a solution better than just talking about it.

Seeking Sister Beatrice

Monday, November 22, 1999, 11:30 am

Ruth told her husband Dave about wanting to seek out her former high school physics teacher as a special way to celebrate turning 50. Since they planned to be in Indiana for Thanksgiving, it seemed like a good time to visit Sister Beatrice, if she could be located.

Ruth started her search by calling her old high school. The woman in the office answering the phone at Divine Mercy had never heard of Sister Mary Beatrice, but suggested that the principal, who had been at the school for 10 years, might be able to help.

After a moment on hold, the kind voice of the principal greeted Ruth. She found Ruth's quest to locate her high school physics teacher, after more than three decades, to be a very noble endeavor.

"Your beloved teacher Sister Mary Beatrice likely no longer goes by that name, since nuns in our order now use their birth names instead of special religious names," the Sister explained. "Do you by chance know her birth name?"

"I have no idea," Ruth responded. "Is there any teacher still at the school who was there 30 years ago and might know?"

"Not that I can think of. Let me give you the phone number for the retirement home where our older sisters live after they stop teaching."

When the principal returned with the number, she made a point of advising Ruth, "If the person answering the phone can't help you, make sure you ask to speak with Sister Kathy. She knows everything about everyone."

Ruth called the phone number for the retirement home, and a woman with a pleasant young voice answered. Ruth explained the details of her seeking Sister Mary Beatrice. Once again, Ruth was asked, "Do you know her birth name?" Ruth again said no.

"Without having that information, I'm afraid I can't help you," the woman responded.

"Okay, thank you. Is Sister Kathy available for me to speak with?" asked Ruth.

"Just a minute," the young woman responded.

After a long pause, a new voice came on the line. "I understand you are trying to find a nun named Sister Mary Beatrice who taught physics at Divine Mercy High School."

"Yes," replied Ruth. "That's correct. I think Sister Beatrice was probably around 40 years old when I knew her in 1967. If so, she would be around 72 now."

"If that's the case, she is probably either living here, or passed away—unless she left our order. Sorry, but we don't have any records here of the former religious names of our residents, since the name changes took place more than 20 years ago."

Sister Kathy continued, "If you'd like, I can

make an announcement to all of our residents during our evening meal tonight. Maybe one of the sisters here used to be called Sister Beatrice, or once knew someone by that name."

Ruth was hopeful as she provided her home phone number and then thanked the sister for her willingness to help.

As she got off of the phone, Ruth prayed, *Dear God, you have put a strong desire on my heart to find Sister Beatrice, so please help someone who knows her to come forward—or somehow give me a new lead.*

That evening, Ruth jumped out of her chair when the phone rang. "I have some information that may or may not be helpful," said Sister Kathy. "One of our newly retired sisters knew a younger nun who taught physics named Sister Noreen Gleason. She thinks her earlier name may have been Sister Beatrice, but she can't be sure."

She continued, "I looked up Sister Noreen Gleason in our order's registry and found that she is still working. The records show she has an unusual assignment. Instead of teaching at a girls' high school or Catholic college, she is teaching physics at the public community college outside Indianapolis. I have a phone number here for her at that college if you want to try calling her tomorrow."

Ruth was thrilled. "Thank you so much! Hopefully Sister Noreen Gleason will either be Sister Beatrice or know who she is."

The next morning, Ruth called the community college and was soon speaking with Sister Noreen. Encouraged by the familiar sounding voice, Ruth asked, "Did you teach physics at Divine Mercy High School in 1967?"

"Yes, I did," the sister replied curiously, and then added, "My name then was Sister Mary Beatrice."

Ruth's heart leapt for joy, and she silently thanked God.

"My name is Ruth Starsky Tanner. I currently live in Michigan and was a physics student of yours in 1967. I have been thinking about my past a lot lately and would very much like to meet with you for coffee or lunch while I am in Indianapolis for Thanksgiving weekend."

"Well, I always enjoy visiting with former students," the sister replied.

They made plans to reunite at a coffee shop the day after Thanksgiving. Ruth could hardly wait.

1. Discover how exciting it is to locate a special teacher from your past.

2. Search persistently, pursuing every lead you get, and always seeking new leads.

The Coffee Shop

Friday, November 26, 1999, 11:30 am

The morning after enjoying a lovely Thanksgiving with her parents, Ruth reminisced, showing them and Dave yearbook photos of herself and Sister Beatrice. Unsure of whether she and her teacher would recognize one another, Ruth carefully studied the nun's countenance in the pictures one last time before she departed for the coffee shop, trying to imagine her face as it would be today—more wrinkled and surrounded with gray hair instead of a nun's habit.

After a 15-minute drive through the lovely suburbs, Ruth was one block away from the meeting spot, just starting to look out her window in search of the coffee shop's sign. Suddenly, a barking dog ran into the street, oblivious to the approaching traffic.

Ruth instinctively slammed on her brakes as the car in front of hers stopped in an instant to avoid hitting the canine. But the relief of avoiding an accident was short-lived—she felt a sudden mini-whiplash accompanied by a bang as the car behind her gently crashed into her bumper.

Ruth took a deep breath, trying to slow her racing heartbeat, and then got out of the car to check on the scene behind her. The other driver emerged as well. Turning to talk with each other, the two women both spoke at the same time, "Are you okay?"

Again simultaneously, they both responded, "Yes, I am," and then grinned at their synchronicity.

Looking closely at the distraught woman with short salt and pepper hair, Ruth recognized her. "Are you Sister Noreen Gleason?" she asked, using the nun's birth name.

The woman's eyes widened. "Yes! Are you Ruth?"

Ruth nodded with a smile, which faded as their eyes shifted to the accident scene. "I can't believe this happened," said Ruth. Examining the two vehicles, Ruth saw that her car appeared to have no damage, and although Sister Noreen's bumper was detached and hanging low on one end, it only had a few scratches.

"I think I have some bungee cords in my trunk that we could use to secure your bumper temporarily," said Ruth.

Sister replied, "That would be great."

Ruth opened her trunk, found the cords, and the two women worked together to get the bumper positioned and secured, impressing a few witnesses who watched from the safety of the nearby sidewalk.

"Thanks for your help," said Sister Noreen. "That should be good enough until I get to a garage later. For now, let's just park behind the coffee shop and go inside to talk as planned."

Ruth agreed.

Once they were seated, the petite woman began, "I am so sorry for hitting your car, Ruth.

Thank goodness your bumper is okay."

"Well," observed Ruth, "That dog ran out so fast, I was lucky not to hit the car in front of me. I'm just glad you are okay, Sister Beatrice—I mean, Sister Noreen.

"Oh dear, I haven't been called Sister Beatrice in decades. It makes me feel young again."

"Speaking of feeling young, I thought you were probably in your 40's when you taught me in 1967, but seeing how young you look now, I must have been mistaken."

"Teenagers always think their teachers are old, especially when they are wearing habits. I am 59 years old now and was 27 when I was your teacher. To be honest, I don't recognize you. I have had thousands of students over the years, and I simply can't remember them all."

Ruth proceeded to explain to Sister Noreen about her desire to celebrate turning 50 by finding and expressing her gratitude to a few people who had made a significant difference in her life. "You helped me to find my passion, Sister. Because of you, I majored in physics in college and went on to become a mechanical engineer. There weren't many women studying these subjects but knowing you and how gifted you were helped me to believe in myself—and know that I could survive and even thrive in science and technology fields. Even if you don't remember teaching me, I want you to know what an important influence you were in my life."

Sister Noreen's eyes began to fill with tears. She couldn't believe Ruth went through the trouble to find her after so many years. She wanted to hear about her life and her work, so Ruth quickly gave her the highlights of her education, her family, and her job. Ruth, in turn, wanted to hear all about the last three decades of Sister Noreen's life as a nun and as a teacher.

"Well, to be honest, I haven't spent *all* of the last three decades as a nun and a teacher. When I was in my mid-30's I went through a sort of life crisis and became very disillusioned. There was talk of a lot of changes coming to our sisterhood, including eliminating habits and religious names. I wasn't sure that I wanted to continue my life as a teaching sister; I had liked wearing a habit and having a religious name. Throughout the bible, the names of people often changed once God had transformed their lives. Abram became Abraham; Jacob became Israel; Simon became Peter; Saul became Paul. I figured if the sisterhood was going to discontinue important traditions and become secularized, I might as well go live and work in the real world.

"So I left the convent and took a job as an environmental engineer with a medium-sized company. I worked there for three years, and found I was disillusioned with the real world as well. I realized that it wasn't my religious name or my habit that was important. What I really missed most was the community of sisters that I had been living with and loving like a family, as well as the important meaningful work we did together—teaching and inspiring teenage girls."

Sister continued, "So I returned to the convent. I was grateful that they welcomed me with open arms, like in the parable of the Prodigal Son. By this time, the nuns' habits and old names were completely gone. I retained my birth name with the title Sister in front of it, and I resumed teaching at both a Catholic high school and Catholic college with a new sense of purpose. A few years ago I was given the opportunity to teach physics at the community college, a challenge that I embraced. Although I have really enjoyed teaching a very broad base of girls and boys, both believers and non-believers, I am seriously considering retiring at the end of this academic year."

Ruth and Sister Noreen talked about God's guiding hand in both of their lives. Neither of them had traveled in a straight line, but always on a zigzag path that brought them to exactly where God wanted them to be, helping and being helped by others.

"Now I remember you, Ruth!" Sister exclaimed. "You are the student who wanted to determine the length of a string that was wrapped around a cylinder. You were so excited when you came back later and told me you had figured out the answer!"

When it was time to go, they hugged one another. "Thank you so much for the lovely visit," the nun said with a tearful smile. "And Ruth, I hope you have a extra special 50th birthday."

1. Realize that the problems that cause you the most difficulty are the ones that teach you lessons that you remember the most.

2. Understand that the path to finding one's true purpose in life is usually not a straight one. Each detour provides valuable experiences that will help later in life.

3. Follow the still small voice that moves you to get in touch with people you have not seen in a while. You never know what's going on in their lives and how your contacting them may be just what you both need.

Preparing for Christmas

Saturday, November 27, 1999, 8:30 am

Driving home to Michigan with Dave the following day, Ruth felt very satisfied about her visit with Sister Noreen. She knew that when God puts a persistent thought on your heart, something you are supposed to do or someone you are supposed to interact with, He always works out a way to make it happen. Ruth's peace and satisfaction were short-lived, however, since she knew life was going to be extra busy at work and at home for the next few weeks. With Dave at the wheel, Ruth had time think about all that still needed to be done in this month before Christmas.

On the forefront of her mind was her job and global concerns about the impact the upcoming millennium would have on all computer systems (a phenomenon referred to as Y2K–short for Year 2000). IT departments at companies around the world had been frantically converting all computer programs from the standard two-digit year date of "99" to the now required four-digit year date of "1999." Without the change, January 1, 2000 would become 01/01/00, which software could interpret as January 1, 1900. The idea of this causing automated scheduling and sequencing problems had the news media in a frenzy with stories of planes potentially falling from the sky, subway trains crashing, and money in bank accounts disappearing.

All of the software that Ruth was responsible for in her department had been converted to be Y2K compliant, but her subordinates were still doing double and triple checks to make sure nothing had been overlooked.

Dave interrupted her thoughts. "Hey Ruth, you know how excited I am about my Wisconsin Badgers making it to the Rose Bowl this year. What do you think about us traveling to Pasadena to see the New Year's game in person?"

Ruth did not immediately reply, thinking Dave's love of sports was clouding his otherwise sound judgment. Dave added, "It would be such an incredible way to start the new millennium!"

Ruth took a close look at her husband, whose eyes were focused on the road. At 55, Dave was still a handsome man–5'10" tall with dark brown hair and eyes, and bushy eyebrows that went upward when he responded to jokes with his hearty laugh. Most of the fifteen extra pounds he carried resided on his mid-section, but at every class reunion, he was still the best-looking guy in the room. Ruth didn't want to disappoint him.

"I know how much you want to go, but I am concerned about Y2K. Since no one really knows what will happen if computer systems go awry, to be on the safe side, I just don't think we should be flying anywhere over New Year's weekend."

Dave, still hopeful, continued, "I understand your concerns, but I really don't think any major harm will come to us if we go, and you know, I'd really love to check this off my bucket list. How about I contact the Wisconsin Alumni Association and see if they have tickets available?"

"Well, Dave," she responded, "I know this event is important to you. Personally I would rather pass on it for this year, and go the next time the Badgers make it to the Rose Bowl. Let's talk about it again once we know if there are any tickets available." Then Ruth said a prayer that God would move Dave to change his mind about Pasadena this year.

As they pulled into the driveway of their home in Michigan, a light snow began to fall, which got them in the mood to begin decorating for Christmas. They went inside, turned the heat up in the house, unpacked the car, put on some Christmas music, and started bringing boxes of holiday decorations up from the basement.

Dave wanted to get the outside decorations up before dark and before too much snow accumulated. Luckily, a reprieve in the snowfall gave him the perfect opportunity. He wrapped garland and white lights around the lamppost and the arbor, placed a lighted star of Bethlehem on the railing above the front porch, and focused a red spotlight on the front door, replacing the Thanksgiving wreath with a Christmas one. Ruth placed lights simulating three candles on the inside of each of the house's eight front windows. Then, she set up automatic timers to control the indoor and outdoor lights.

With darkness setting in, the snowfall resumed, just in time for the couple to take a romantic evening stroll to the curb. There they appreciated the warmth the Christmas decorations and lights added to the outside appearance of their red brick Williamsburg colonial house.

After dinner, they sat down to review, revise, and finalize the annual Christmas letter they had drafted together before Thanksgiving. For them, this was more than a typical holiday greeting—it was a one-page printed summary of the ups and downs of their family's past year, with as much humor thrown in as possible. Ruth kept a binder titled "A Chronicle of Blessings," containing all of their Christmas letters since 1974, the year their youngest child Kate had been born. It was their precious 25-year family history.

On Sunday, Christmas carols filled the air during the inside house decorating activities. Ruth danced around placing decorations throughout the main rooms on the first floor. Dave set up the tree, put on its lights, and spiraled gold ribbons and bows around the branches. Then together, while looking out at the lake and viewing the snow-covered trees and rooftops of the homes in the distance, they put ornaments on the tree, recalling memories that each trinket evoked from Christmases past.

Monday after work, Dave and Ruth addressed envelopes for about 70 cards and slipped a copy of their new Christmas letter inside. They reminisced, rereading last year's cards received from their friends and family, so they could include a personalized, hand-written comment. It was always sad to delete from the list the names of those who had passed away since last Christmas.

On Tuesday and Wednesday, they focused on holiday shopping. Dave took the lead on purchasing and wrapping gifts for Ruth and his parents, while Ruth took care of presents for everyone else, welcoming any hints on preferences that the family members had to offer.

Ruth knew that buying Christmas gifts for her was particularly difficult for Dave, especially with her birthday being on December 22nd. Regardless of how busy they were with holiday preparations on that day, he always tried to make time to take her out for a nice birthday dinner and gifted her with one thoughtful surprise. This year would probably be no different.

Ruth's Journal

1. Talk through issues of concern and disagreement you have as a couple. It may take several sessions of dialog before you find a solution that you are both comfortable with.

2. Take time in the midst of the holiday rush to enjoy your family traditions, and do all holiday tasks in a spirit of anticipation, happiness, and love.

An Unexpected Trip

Thursday, December 2, 1999, 5:30 pm

After work, Ruth breathed a contented sigh of relief as she sipped a cup of hot chocolate with mini-marshmallows. She admired the Christmas decorations and lighted tree, listened to the Christmas carols softly playing on the stereo, and waited for Dave to come home for dinner. They had been working so hard the entire week decorating, shopping, and getting the Christmas cards mailed out; they deserved to take the night off.

Dave walked through the door with a big grin on his face and asked, "How would you like to travel with me to Germany eight days from now?"

Ruth quickly swallowed her sip. "What?"

"My boss asked Nate and me to attend a trade show at the Messe in Hannover, Germany, that runs the week of December 13th. I asked if I could bring my wife along, since she speaks German and could be a big help to us. He replied, 'Fine, she can share your hotel room, but she has to pay for her own food, ground transportation, and airfare.'"

Then he squealed, "Ruth, can you believe it?"

Ruth looked at Dave with her mouth gaping, as she tried to comprehend what he had just relayed during his excited monolog. Then she tried to determine if such a crazy, spontaneous idea was even feasible. A series of thoughts ran through Ruth's mind and out of her mouth.

"Well, as hectic as December usually is, we are actually caught up with the Christmas tasks at home. Since Ma is making the Tanner Christmas cookies this year, all we really have left to do is finish getting a few remaining gifts purchased and wrapped." She paused as if to switch gears. "And at work, Y2K preparations for my team seem to be on schedule. I still have seven days of vacation that I need to use by Christmas or I will lose them. However, I absolutely have to be at the office to run a critical meeting Thursday, December 16th."

Grabbing the calendar that was affixed to the refrigerator door by two strong magnets, Ruth continued with growing excitement, "We could fly out Friday evening, December 10th, arrive on December 11th, get the lay of the land on Sunday, December 12th, and attend the trade show at the Messe in Hannover on the 13th and 14th. I could fly home on Wednesday, the 15th, to get back to work for my meeting. You and Nate could fly home at the end of the week, since you should know your way around Hannover just fine by then. You know, I have never been in Germany for Weihnachtsmarkt—the Christmas Market— and I have always wanted to see one. I'll have to ask my boss for the vacation time off, but it's only three work days and I am sure he'll say yes."

"Ruth, I am so glad that you want to go," Dave said, giving her a warm embrace. "I love traveling overseas with you. It seems we always have adventures that we talk about for years."

First thing in the morning, Ruth got her boss's approval for the vacation days and called Dave. His colleague, Nate, wanted to fly out a day later on Saturday, December 11th, and both men could fly back together on Friday, December 17th. Dave spoke with the department secretary and then phoned Ruth an hour later.

Knowing that Ruth loved any chance to save money, Dave started, "I have some amazing news! Since your coach airfare was less than half of a first class ticket, my boss has approved having the company cover coach tickets for both of us instead of just a first class ticket for me."

"That's wonderful!" Ruth exclaimed.

"Yes, it is. But, the secretary ran into a snag trying to make travel arrangements so late. Apparently every hotel near Hannover is booked because of the trade show, so the closest available hotel she could find was in Hamburg, a 90-minute trip by speed train. She has gone ahead and booked us all flights to and from Hamburg."

"That's okay with me. I'm fine with staying in Hamburg," Ruth said. "I didn't realize that Hannover was commutable from Hamburg."

"Hey," noted Dave, "I know you were a foreign exchange student at the University of Hamburg a few years before we met. Maybe you can show me the campus and where you lived if we have some time." He continued, "Oh, and Ruth, with this big trip planned, I am fine with not going to Pasadena for the Rose Bowl this year."

Ruth hung up the phone and sat staring at it. Not only had her final Y2K concern been addressed, but also next week, through an unbelievable twist of fate, she would actually be returning to Hamburg, Germany. She wondered if, after three decades, her dear old friend Karl Mensch was still living in that city so that she could thank him for making a difference in her life. But with the reality of this possible meeting setting in, a vain part of her didn't want to look for him; she preferred to have her ex-boyfriend remember her as a cute, thin 19-year old, rather than see her now heavier and older. Then she thought, *Chances are, he's heavier and looks older, too. If I don't seize this rare opportunity to search for him while we're in Hamburg, I may always regret it.*

~~~~~

A week later, Dave and Ruth were on a flight to Germany. This trip was very different from the last time she had made the overnight flight across the Atlantic to Hamburg 30 years earlier. As she dozed on the plane, her mind went back to her days as a college student and the adventures she had experienced overseas.

1. Plan a work trip that also contains some elements of fun whenever you can.

2. Go with the flow when changes to your travel arrangements occur. Often things work out for the best.

3. Don't let concerns about not looking good enough keep you from doing anything that God puts on your heart to do.

PART II

> "Have I not commanded you? Be strong and courageous. Do not be afraid; do not be discouraged, for the Lord your God will be with you wherever you go."
> ~ Joshua 1:9

A Foreign Exchange Student

April 1969

It was a cold day in Hamburg, Germany, when Ruth Starsky disembarked from the first plane ride of her life. Just nineteen years old, she was the youngest of fifteen foreign exchange students from her American university who would be attending Universität Hamburg. When Ruth was first invited to be part of the program, she knew that neither she nor her parents had the $1000 required for her four-month stay overseas—a ten-week school term ending in July followed by six weeks of free time for travel or other summer activities. Fortunately, she remembered that her Grandma Sophie had contributed money every birthday and Christmas to a savings account for each grandchild since birth, and Ruth's account had accumulated $1100 that she could use for the trip.

The family Ruth had been assigned to live with consisted of Frau Hoffmann, a middle-aged professional woman who spoke English and worked for Lufthansa Airlines, and her elderly mother (affectionately called Oma [Grandma]) who spoke no English and was always at home. Frau Hoffmann's adult son Rolf spoke English, lived nearby, and came to visit their second story flat for dinner every week or so. Although the home was small and included only a living room, kitchen, two bedrooms, one bathroom, and a tiny study where Ruth would sleep, she felt welcomed by the family's kindness and knew it would be a supportive home away from home.

It took her a few days to adjust to everyone calling her 'Root,' which is how the Germans pronounce Ruth. Once classes began, keeping up with the coursework and learning to speak German was a real challenge for her. Thirteen of the fifteen foreign exchange students were third or fourth year German majors. Ruth and a boy from New York were the only sophomores in the group and consequently were the poorest at speaking German. Ruth ended up employing three strategies for learning the language: speaking at home with the Hoffmanns, watching German TV, and interacting with German college students.

At home, Ruth spent the most time with Oma, a frail, crotchety, stooped-over woman who seldom smiled. Oma took a liking to her, and patiently listened as Ruth painstakingly put together simple German sentences to explain what had happened during her adventures at the University each day. Oma would rephrase each sentence as necessary using the correct pronunciation and grammar. Then Ruth would repeat it and in that way learn to speak Hochdeutsch ['high' German], the formal German taught in school without slang.

When it came to learning German from TV, Ruth's favorite show was 'Friedrich Feuerstein

[Fred Flintstone],' which was a dubbed version of the familiar American cartoon series 'The Flintstones.' The storylines were simple and the dialog was relatively easy to follow, containing useful everyday conversations. Ruth took notes, jotting down phrases she wanted to remember and use in the future.

Most of the fourteen exchange students, who traveled with her, spent a lot of their free time together speaking in English, talking about their German host families and adjustment issues. While Ruth found this familiar and comforting, she was in Hamburg for only one term and intended to completely immerse herself in the German culture. Ruth wanted to spend time trying to converse with German students even if her German skills were subpar.

After about three days of various German culture and speaking classes, including a 'German for Foreigners' course, Ruth decided to check out some of the physics classes on campus. Studying the campus map she had been given on the first day, she couldn't find any building marked "Physik." In the distance, a lanky, dark-haired figure was walking toward Ruth. As he got closer, they made eye contact, which gave her confidence to approach the German student.

"Do you speak English?" Ruth asked, hoping for an affirmative reply.

"Nein. Nur ein bisschen [Only a little]," he responded. "Sprechen Sie Deutsch?"

"Nur ein bisschen," Ruth replied. She didn't want to make a fool out of herself and her vocabulary was limited. But she decided to just try her best to communicate. Pointing to her campus map, she asked in halting German where the

Physics Department was located.

Looking at the map, the student shook his head and answered, "Nicht hier [Not here]" Then he pointed to a spot about four inches away from the paper and said, "Hier."

Ruth looked disappointed. Her campus map showed the university's main campus but not the more remote south campus, which is where she deduced the Physics Department must be located. "Danke," she replied, exasperated, and started to walk away.

"Moment, bitte. Mein Auto ist dort [Just a minute, please. My car is there]," he said, indicating a nearby cluster of vehicles. Then he pointed to Ruth, pointed to himself, and imitated an arcing driving motion of two hands on a steering wheel.

Ruth realized that he was offering to drive her to the Physics Department. Getting into a car with a stranger was never a good idea, especially in a foreign country with no one familiar around for her to report where she was going. She silently prayed, *God, should I do this?* She felt a sense of peace come over her. Then she thought, *If this student can take me to the right building now, I can probably find my way later to the nearest public transportation to get home.*

"Okay. To the physics building. Danke," Ruth decided gratefully. As they walked toward a very small orange car, she introduced herself. "Ich heiße Ruth [I am called Ruth]."

"Ich heiße Karl." The tall blue-eyed student smiled warmly as he opened the car door for her.

The drive took about ten minutes. Ruth did not understand everything that Karl said, except for the fact that he was studying geology and 'sport' and wanted to be a teacher. Ruth told him she was from America, studying physics and German, and was only at Universität Hamburg for one term.

When they arrived at the Physics building, Ruth thanked Karl, got out of the car, and headed inside.

Seeing some students filing into a large tiered science lecture hall, Ruth decided to follow them into the class to see what the course was like. She found a seat in the back of the room, which gave her a bird's eye view of the professor, the blackboard, and the backs of the other students.

The professor began speaking quickly and the students around her were paying strict attention. Ruth had no idea what he was saying but when she heard a new word repeated several times, she looked it up in her pocket-sized German-English dictionary.

Oh, he's talking about angular velocity, Ruth thought to herself, and this was confirmed as the professor started to quickly write an equation on the board, and then another, and then another. He talked as he wrote, and though she didn't understand all of what he was saying, the equations that flowed as the chalk marks filled the board made perfect sense. Ruth smiled with understanding and joy. *It's true; mathematics really is a universal language.*

Pausing from the theoretical discussion, the professor motioned to a young man, whom Ruth assumed was his teaching assistant, to bring a rotating stool and some other items to the center of the teaching platform. He then performed a demonstration on angular velocity, which was quite impressive. As the stool's rotation slowed to a stop, the students started knocking loudly on their desks, increasing the speed of the raps to a crescendo.

The action startled Ruth—until she realized that rapping on their desks was the students' way of showing approval for a professor! That alternative to applause was something you would never see in America.

~~~~~

The following day, Ruth went to a local department store near the university searching for a bathing cap. The store had one she liked but it was not available in her size. The store clerk explained that they had another location not far away by train that might carry her size. Ruth seemed interested, so the clerk called and was happy to report that they indeed had the cap in stock. Ruth got on the train following the clerk's directions.

After traveling a few stops, the conductor asked for Ruth's pass. Conductors did occasional random checks to make sure everyone had valid tickets, and with her monthly student pass in hand, Ruth was not concerned.

The conductor's passive demeanor suddenly changed to one of anger as he knew what Ruth didn't—she had traveled out of the district that was valid for her pass. He hollered at her in rapid German for not purchasing the right ticket and told her she had to get off the train at the next stop and pay a fine immediately. Otherwise, she could go to jail.

As tears filled her eyes, Ruth tried to apologize for her ignorance, but the man kept yelling and refused to listen. As he filled out a violation form, she asked him how much money she needed to pay the fine. Luckily she had enough, and he calmed down when he saw the Deutschmarks she pulled from her purse. He gave her the paper as a receipt, and then, switching to a totally calm professional tone, he told her that with it, she could legally travel anywhere else in the city for the rest of the day. There was a rule that you could not pay more than one train fine on any given day.

Hearing that, Ruth took a deep breath, grateful to know she would not be locked up in a foreign prison. Feeling relieved, she got on the next train continuing to her destination, where she found the bathing cap she wanted. Factoring in the violation fine, it was the most expensive bathing cap she had ever purchased.

1. Don't be afraid of making mistakes when you try to speak a new language. Be humble, forget about your ego, and you will improve over time.

2. Be grateful for people who care enough to correct you privately when you make an error.

3. Pray before you take an action that seems risky. If you feel a peace, proceed with caution.

4. Remember to breathe deeply when someone is yelling at you and you feel scared. Most of the time, things are not as bad as they seem.

A Different Way of Thinking

Early May 1969

A week later, Ruth ran into Karl on campus, and they stopped to talk. She was glad to see the friendly German student who had previously gone out of his way to help her. They were both finished with classes for the day, and he invited her to get some coffee.

"I don't drink coffee, but I would be happy to join you anyway," said Ruth.

As they found a table at a nearby café, Ruth ordered Ananassaft [pineapple juice], her favorite fruit juice that was readily available at most coffee shops in Germany. She told him all about the physics class she had attended, and then asked him to tell her about himself.

She was surprised to learn that he was 24, which was older than undergraduate students she had known at home. Ruth explained that she had skipped the third grade and finished high school when she was 17. She was 19 now and planned to finish college in two more years.

Karl described how in Germany, students

were usually 19 when they finished high school, and the boys were then required to spend time in government service either as a soldier or as a policeman. He had chosen the latter. For hobbies, he liked coaching boys' soccer, repairing car engines, and working with electronics. Ruth noticed that his hands were large and strong, like her grandfather's.

When Ruth stood up to head home, Karl commented, "I am on a committee that is planning a spring celebration on campus. Would you like to come to a meeting tomorrow afternoon and meet some of my friends?"

Ruth replied that she would think about it, and he wrote down the meeting time and campus location on a piece of paper.

"If I decide to come, I will see you there," Ruth responded.

She went home and talked with Oma about the invitation. "It sounds like fun," said Oma, who was encouraging. Ruth agreed, smiling. Even though Oma, true to her nature, did not crack a smile, Ruth knew this dear old woman was smiling on the inside.

The next day, Ruth successfully navigated to the meeting location that was written on Karl's paper. She found Karl, who was happy to see her, and together they volunteered to help decorate the hall where the celebration and dance would be held. The other students—both guys and girls—were all friendly to this petite American girl who was Karl's new acquaintance.

Some of them were studying to be teachers and a comment from one young man struck Ruth as quite memorable. He explained that he wanted to teach biology and that the practicums were known to be very difficult; he had to demonstrate that he could teach biology at all levels—basic through advanced—before he could receive his teacher's license.

"What will you do if you don't pass the practicums?" asked Ruth.

"Then I will just have to settle for becoming a doctor," he replied.

Ruth was quite surprised by this comment. "But isn't it harder to become a doctor than to become a teacher?" she asked, knowing that was certainly true in America.

"Here in Germany, teachers are considered to be among the most educated and intelligent people in society, are highly respected, and are required to know more than people working in other professions. The government pays them very well. Teachers are the intelligentsia who educate the minds that are the future of our country."

Ruth admitted to herself that teachers had been a huge influence in her life, but she never felt like American society in general had a great deal of respect for the profession, and American teachers certainly were not paid well. There was even a saying she had heard that conveyed a sentiment of disrespect: 'Those who can, do. Those who can't, teach.' She thought to herself, *Perhaps other parts of the world have a different way of thinking. Maybe German values are closer to those of Plato, whose utopia was a land ruled by a philosopher king, a lover of wisdom and intelligence.*

One student who had studied for a year at a college in America had this observation:

"Education is very different here in Germany. There are no tests, no grades, only classes, so it's difficult to say if you're doing well or not. Here, when a student registers for classes, the courses are put on your record and you receive credit. If you participate or not, it doesn't really matter to anybody, but in the long run, not participating can hurt you. At the end of your university career, a group of professors looks at the courses you've signed up for and determines what you should know. Then, for four months, they give you written examinations, have discussions with you, make you give speeches, explanations, and in general, determine if you are a well-rounded, well-educated person with extra strength in a specific area. You either pass, and earn your degree, or fail. If you fail, you can study longer or do anything you wish before repeating the evaluation. If you fail a second time, you're finished—with no degree."

He continued, "In many ways the system is better here. Instead of cramming for frequent tests and forgetting the material a short time later, Germans focus on learning for a lifetime. Students don't have nervous breakdowns over grades and somehow they seem to know much more about many more things. People study longer here and the university students are older than those in America. Also since liberal arts are valued here, there is not the pressure to go into technical fields that is so prevalent in America."

Intrigued, Ruth now understood why the trip coordinator had to make arrangements with each of the German professors to administer special end-of-term tests for the foreign exchange students—they didn't normally give any final exams!

The group's conversation turned to the topic of attitudes about sex. Ruth commented that every block in Hamburg had nude magazines on display, something she would never see at home. A female student explained, "Most people here have a very casual attitude about sex, and enjoy it like they would a sport or other hobby. Once two people marry, it is expected that they stay faithful to each other, unless they agree to have an open marriage. What do you believe, Ruth?"

She replied, "While some people in America think that way, I view sex as something so intimate, so special, that I want to experience it for the first time on my honeymoon with a man I love, who has pledged to be with me for a lifetime. Right now I am being faithful to the man I will marry someday, even though I don't know him yet. The people I know who have sex before marriage have the worries of unplanned pregnancies, sexual diseases, and emotional distress. Most of them are a mess. I don't judge them; it's their choice. That's just not something I want."

"But Ruth, when you are in love, it is hard not to have sex," said another student.

Ruth considered telling the group that she had made a vow to God when she was 16 to remain a virgin until the day she married. Instead she decided to keep her response more secular in tone, saying, "My experience with love has been that if you agree ahead of time to keep your clothes on and go no further than kissing, it is much easier to not have sex. Substituting a different physical activity, like dancing, can be fun and is much safer."

"Ruth," said Karl, "you certainly have a different way of thinking." The others nodded in agreement.

Ruth's Journal

1. "Seek first to understand, then to be understood." This key phrase is based on the 'Prayer of St. Francis.'

2. Be respectful of the various beliefs and attitudes of others. You increase the likelihood that they will try to be respectful of your beliefs, even if they don't agree.

3. Give teachers the recognition they deserve—even if our society doesn't.

4. Discuss ahead of time, the boundaries you want to set on your romantic relationships, so you don't get swept up in the moment and do something you will later regret.

Family Time

Mid-May 1969

Ruth spent a lot of her time studying in the Hoffmann flat. Frau Hoffmann was always cordial and thought it was important that she and her son Rolf take Ruth on a few weekend excursions to supplement her university education. Sometimes Oma came as well.

The first was a trip to the Reeperbahn in St. Pauli, Hamburg's world-famous red light entertainment district for sailors. An amazing variety of people filled the streets from well-dressed businessmen to homely streetwalkers. The first stop was the Zillertal, a Bavarian drinking place with traditional lederhosen-clad musicians and waitresses with puffy sleeves and full skirts.

The following morning they went to Altes Land [Old Country], a beautiful area on the Elbe River that had 500-year-old farmhouses and large orchards. There were lots of birds and wildlife, plus sheep and shepherds. It was all very slow-paced and relaxing, a sharp contrast to the bustling city where they lived.

Another excursion was a bit more harrowing. With Rolf driving and Frau Hoffmann in the passenger seat, they took Ruth to Berlin. The city had been divided into West Berlin and East Berlin after World War II, and they had to drive from Hamburg through West Germany, and then through a portion of East Germany in order to get to West Berlin. There were checkpoints that had to be passed from West Germany to East Germany, and then from East Germany to West Berlin.

Ruth was transfixed by the double row of fencing and barbed wire 100 feet apart with mine fields in between that separated the West from the East, especially at the borders. While they were approaching a checkpoint, she noticed a guard in the tower above the barbed wire and got out her camera to take a photo. Through the rear view mirror Rolf spotted Ruth in the back seat, and immediately shouted, "No, NO, put that camera away!" Frau Hoffmann swung around and slapped the camera to the floor.

"Are you trying to get us all arrested?" rebuked Frau Hoffmann sternly. "Taking pictures is forbidden by the East German government, especially photos of towers, armed guards, and barbed wire fences. Keep your camera hidden in your bag until we are safely inside West Berlin."

Ruth was ashamed at her own naiveté. She was just now beginning to understand the real impact splitting Germany after World War II had on the German people. Those living in the West had freedom, jobs, and prosperity. Those living in the communist East were poor, controlled by the government, and unable to leave. Traveling through East Germany to get to West Berlin required permission and they had to stay on the autobahn without getting off until they arrived in West Berlin. Forms had to be filled out, passports examined and paperwork at each checkpoint was time-stamped so no detours could be taken. Mirrors were placed under the vehicle for inspection. At one checkpoint, the East German guard had everyone get out of the car. While Rolf attended to paperwork, the guard told Frau Hoffmann to lift out the back seat. She tried but couldn't figure out how to do it. So she removed the car manual from the glove box, handed it to the guard, and very sweetly told him he was welcome to check under the back seat if he could figure out how to remove it. He finally just waved them through. The oppression of communism was palpable.

The city of West Berlin was a mix of bombed-out areas, old structures that had survived the war, and new buildings. Shops, outdoor cafés, and beautiful boulevards were bustling with upbeat residents and visitors. However, just looking at the Berlin Wall and knowing the extreme deprivation and tyranny that existed on the other side cast an ominous cloud of despair, which touched even the free side of Berlin.

The ride home was non-eventful. Ruth didn't realize how tense she was until they passed through the last checkpoint entering West Germany, when she breathed a sigh of relief.

~ ~ ~ ~ ~

Ruth had been writing home once or twice a week, and always looked forward to receiving mail from her parents and siblings. One day she was having a touch of homesickness and she wrote in her letter, *I am so tired of hearing and reading nothing but German. I really want to hear your voices, if only for a few minutes, so I have arranged with Frau Hoffmann to reimburse her so I can make a three-minute long distance call home. It will be on your anniversary* *at 6:00 pm your time, which is midnight my time. Long distance calls are very expensive, but the phone rates here are lowest at that time— $7.00 for three minutes.*

Frau Hoffmann and Ruth stayed up late on the appointed day to make the call. The connection was so clear that Ruth laughed and cried simultaneously—it was like her family was in the same room with her, instead of thousands of miles away. Not knowing who was happier, she or her parents, Ruth ended the call saying, "Happy Anniversary, Mom and Dad. I carry all of you with me in my heart, everywhere I go."

~~~~~

The next day, Karl called Ruth, saying his parents wanted to invite her over for dinner the following night to meet them, his younger brother Johann, and Johann's fiancée Petra. Ruth was happy to accept, and looked forward to it.

She and Karl had gone out on two dates already. The first was a walk along the Elbe River and a boat tour of Hamburg and the harbor. The second was a walk through the city's botanical gardens called 'Planten un Blomen [Plants and Flowers].' Both dates had been fun with plenty of time for conversation. Each time when he brought her back to the Hoffmann's home, Karl had given her a wink, a smile, and a warm handshake.

As he had done with the earlier dates, Karl picked her up in his 1959 Lloyd automobile so she didn't have to take public transportation. Frau Hoffmann and Oma, having met Karl a few weeks earlier, chatted with him while Ruth gathered her purse and the modest bouquet of flowers she had purchased for Karl's mother.

When they arrived at his building, they

climbed one flight of stairs and entered the family's flat. Ruth was surprised at how much larger their home was on the inside than it looked on the outside. Karl's mom was the sweetest woman and she made Ruth feel right at home. His dad was a little gruff and formal at first, but soon was smiling and telling jokes. Johann was shorter, younger, and better looking than Karl. He had not gone to college and instead was about to start a job with an insurance company in a town south of Frankfurt, more than 500 kilometers [300 miles] away. When Johann talked about the upcoming wedding, it was obvious he was totally captivated by his pretty bride-to-be, Petra.

Over a delicious dinner, Ruth told everyone about her phone call home, and then described each of her five siblings, telling some funny stories about the Starsky family, their polka band, and the fun they had together, especially on holidays. Karl's parents were surprised to discover that little Ruth played a large piano accordion, which was twice the size of the small, locally popular, button box concertina accordion.

When it was time to leave, Karl's mom gave her a hug and insisted, "You must come and visit us again some time."

Karl drove Ruth home, and opened the car door for her. She climbed the first step leading up to the front door and turned around facing him, her eyes now closer to his.

"I really enjoyed meeting your family," she said with a smile.

"I think they like you almost as much as I do." He smiled back.

After gazing into each other's eyes for a moment, he gently cupped her face in his hands and, sensing no resistance, he softly kissed her.

Silently Ruth turned and walked up the remaining steps, her heart racing. She slowly entered the old front door, glancing back still smiling to say goodnight—and then danced up the long staircase that led to the Hoffmann flat.

Ruth's Journal

1. Appreciate personal freedom, especially if you are lucky enough never to have experienced time without it.

2. Savor the ordinary time you spend with your family. When you are no longer with them, you realize nothing is more precious.

3. Spend time with the family of the person you are dating. Sharing food and funny family stories strengthens the foundation of your relationship as a couple.

Car Trouble

Early June 1969

One warm Saturday, Karl wanted to take Ruth on a road trip an hour north of the city to show her a scenic spot. It was a beautiful sunny day and they both were happy to take a break from their schoolwork. The drive on the autobahn passed idyllic landscapes as they chatted about their plans for the summer.

Suddenly, the car's engine stopped running. Karl was in shock and focused all his attention on safely pulling the vehicle over to the side of the road as it coasted to a stop.

"What happened? What's wrong?" Ruth asked in a concerned voice.

"I don't know," mumbled Karl, as he got out of the car and opened the hood. Ruth hopped out of the vehicle as well, and peered into the open engine compartment with him.

"Oh, Scheiße [shit]! The belt broke." He pulled out the severed belt and held it in his hand. "I don't have a replacement with me and we are about 15 kilometers [9 miles] from the next autobahn exit."

Ruth looked at the surrounding countryside

and felt truly stranded. "Should we wait for someone to stop and help, or hitchhike a ride?"

"Let me think a minute," pondered Karl. "Is there anything here that I can use to get it started?" After rifling through the trunk, he started to speak, "I don't see any..." and then he stopped mid-sentence, staring at Ruth's neck. "Your scarf, your nylon scarf! Can I use it to fix the car?" She removed the inexpensive sheer nylon scarf tied around her neck, and handed it to him.

"Of course, but how is that going to help?"

"Your scarf appears to be very fragile, but nylon when twisted is actually quite strong." Karl folded the scarf in half along the diagonal, rolled it and then twisted it a dozen times into a cord-like piece. He compared its length to the broken belt, relieved that it was several inches longer, and jerked on it with both hands in an opposing motion, to confirm that it wouldn't break. Then, after routing it on the side of the engine along the path where the belt had been, he tied a strong knot.

"Do you think this will really work?" Ruth wondered.

"I don't know. You pray and I will turn the key," said Karl. "Eins, zwei, drei [One, two, three]!" Ruth marveled as her scarf quickly rotated around at a steady rate while the motor purred. They both shouted in delight.

Karl spoke urgently as he jumped out of the car to close the hood, "Get in quickly. I don't know how long the scarf will last!"

They made it to the next exit, found a garage and bought a new belt. The mechanic was amazed by the makeshift belt fabricated out of a sheer white scarf, which was now totally blackened from its useful service. He praised Karl for his ingenuity.

Ruth thanked God for moving her to wear the scarf that day, for inspiring Karl to use it to make a belt for the car, and for keeping them safe so far from home.

1. Believe that when you have a problem, a solution may be right in front of you, if you look around at what is available with an open mind.

2. Realize that every unfortunate situation that occurs in your life is a challenge that can make you stronger.

Polterabend

Mid-June 1969

The following week, Johann and Petra's wedding was at hand. Karl had not invited Ruth to the wedding, but he had asked her to come to Polterabend ['noisy evening'], the traditional wedding custom festivity held the night before the wedding at the bride's family's home. Guests break porcelain dishes in front of the door to symbolize the end of all possible bad luck for the couple, and then enter the house for a party.

Petra's mother was German and her father was Polish, so every time a toast was made, the German word, "Prost [Cheers]!" and the Polish phrase "Na zdrowie [To your health]!" both rang out. Petra's father was pleased to hear that Ruth's last name was Starsky and that she liked to polka. A good collection of records kept everyone dancing with everyone else. Ruth and Karl spent some time circulating separately, and she was very comfortable introducing herself to the interesting family members and friends who were there.

Taking a break from dancing, Ruth sipped a drink as she scanned the dancers in the cramped quarters. None of the men appeared to have a strong leading hand that expertly guided his partner around the dance floor like her father did. Her eyes stopped on Karl dancing with a cute fair-haired girl who had come late to the party. Just then, Frau Mensch came over to Ruth and explained, "Karl is dancing with Natalie, his ex-fiancé."

"Oh!" Ruth replied, "Karl did mention to me that he had been engaged once, but he didn't go into any details."

Frau Mensch went on to share, "Natalie is 23. She's a nice person but is often nervous and insecure. She ended their engagement a year ago because she was afraid and not ready to get married. Now I hear she wants Karl back again." Frau Mensch went on to say, "Since he has come to know you, Ruth, Karl has realized how much better and easier it is to be with someone who is self-confident, can get along with people, and can think for herself." Ruth really appreciated his mom's kind words.

Later on, Karl danced with Ruth and explained that Natalie was furious because he would not take her back again. He had told Natalie there was no reason for her to leave the party, however, since she knew many of the people there. She had left anyway.

The next day, Ruth spent the afternoon with some of her exchange student friends. Soon after she returned home, Karl phoned frantically asking her if she could quickly get ready and come to the wedding. He explained that he had not invited her originally thinking his family would prefer if he came to the wedding alone to focus on his best man duties. Besides, his brother and parents had only met with Ruth once before Polterabend, so she was just an acquaintance to them. But as it turned out, after Polterabend, both the bride's parents and his own parents were surprised she wasn't at the wedding, chastising Karl, "Where's Ruth? Why didn't you bring her?" He continued, "The early arriving guests keep asking for the pretty, smiling, American girl who was at Polterabend; so Ruth, you must come now, *please*."

With help from Frau Hoffmann, Ruth was able to make it to the wedding. The short civil service and small reception at a nearby Lokal [restaurant and bar] were quite different from the large church weddings that were a tradition in the Starsky family. Johann and Petra were very happy—and so were Herr and Frau Mensch. As his brother's best man, Karl looked handsome in his wedding attire—especially when he pulled Ruth onto the dance floor.

1. Know that small weddings can be just as festive as large ones.

2. Make an effort to circulate independently at gatherings when your date must attend to guests.

Summary Adventures

July 1969

As the school term was about to end, the 15 foreign exchange students decided to host a huge Fourth of July American picnic as a thank you celebration for their German families and friends. Because the dad of one of the boys was in the US Air Force, he was able to get American food and sports equipment donated or loaned from the US Air Force Base, which was two hours from Hamburg.

When two of the boys drove to the base to pick up the party supplies, they said it was like being back home in the United States—American cheeseburgers, money, music, slang, cars, everything. The people there were quite obliging, providing more than $2500 worth of supplies—loaning US flags and sports equipment like footballs, baseballs, bats, and mitts; plus donating food like hot dogs, hamburgers, buns, American pickles, baked beans, and Heinz ketchup.

On the day of the picnic, Frau Hoffmann was in Italy and Oma didn't want to attend. However, Rolf came with his girlfriend, and Karl and his parents were able to come as well. Although plans for the picnic by the water had to be scrapped due to rainy weather, luckily the Americans had a back-up plan. They were able to move the celebration to the basement of a church five miles away, where there were two rec rooms and a kitchen.

The students started the hamburgers cooking, opened the beer keg, and laid out a spread of fried chicken, potato salad, American pickles, American baked beans, pies, cakes, and cookies. The Germans couldn't believe it. They all wanted to know where they could buy the baked beans, pickles, and the 'thick' American ketchup. Ruth's contributions of her mom's cheesecake and potato salad were also a big hit, even though she had to use substitutes for several ingredients not available in Hamburg. While two students took turns playing a guitar, an American girl led the singing of American songs and Karl led the singing of German songs.

Later the sky cleared, and the sun dried things out enough for the picnickers to go outside for a baseball game. Initially it was chaotic trying to teach the Germans how to play, but they learned very quickly, with Karl easily standing out as the best athlete. What Ruth was really amazed at, however, was Karl's dad, Herr Mensch, who reminded her of her own father. He did an excellent job both at bat and in the field, much better than most of the American boys— and it was the first time he had ever played!

All in all, the celebration was a huge success. Although it was not the same as being in America for the Fourth of July, it felt wonderful to celebrate overseas the holiday of American freedom, sharing traditions from home, and giving thanks for the kindness of new foreign friends.

~ ~ ~ ~ ~

Two days later, the Americans took a boat to the island of Helgoland and then went camping on Sylt, the largest German island in the North Sea.

Some of the students invited German friends to come to the island, thinking it would be wise to have them there in case any problems arose. Ruth was glad that Karl was able to come. The other American students knew and liked him, and joked during the ferry ride to the island that Karl was the reason Ruth's German language skills now surpassed their own. Sylt was 280 kilometers [168 miles] north of Hamburg, almost to Denmark, and the students were all ready for an adventure.

The white sand of the island was amazing and everyone enjoyed sunbathing and playing volleyball on the beach. Some tried swimming but not for too long as the water in the North Sea was very cold. As evening approached, they all sat together and watched the beautiful sunset. Then one of the students suggested that they all go skinny dipping once it got dark.

As one by one, each student agreed to go, Ruth said laughing, "Not me. The water's too cold and I have no desire to see all of you naked." Then she turned to Karl and commented, "If you want to go, don't let me stop you."

Karl laughed and replied, "I'd rather stay here with you. Besides, I need to talk with you about something."

After they found a place to sit that distanced themselves from the sights and sounds of the skinny dipping group, Ruth could sense Karl was about to tell her something important.

"I have a daughter," he began. Ruth stopped breathing for an instant, and then tried to keep her expression neutral. "Her name is Sabina and she is two years old. Her mother really liked me, pursued me, and we had casual sex several times. I was very stupid—she told me she was on the pill; but she had stopped taking it hoping to get pregnant and have me marry her. I didn't love her, didn't want to marry her, and felt totally duped and manipulated. I resented what she did and couldn't stand the sight of her or the baby. I haven't seen them since the baby was born."

"Oh, wow." Ruth took a moment to take in the news. Then, concerned for the fatherless child, she asked, "Are you sending money to support the baby?"

"No, I'm still a student, living at home with my parents, hardly able to provide for myself, let alone anyone else. I assume they are both still living with her parents. I want nothing to do with them."

Ruth was silent. Karl had seemed smart and responsible and someone who loved being around kids. Resenting the young woman he believed had tricked him might be understandable, but rejecting his own daughter and feeling no urge to help support her were actions that Ruth did not view as very noble.

Ruth replied simply, "I know it was hard for you to tell me this. I'm glad you did. I'll pray that you have wisdom to do the right thing going forward. Remember, Sabina is completely innocent, so don't blame or punish her for your mistake."

At that point they could hear all the skinny dippers coming out of the water and getting dressed. It was time to rejoin the group for a bonfire. She kissed Karl on the cheek, stood up, and brushed off the sand from her shorts. Deep inside, she thought, *That's why no matter how much I love someone, until we are married, I will never do more than kissing. It keeps life much simpler!*

~~~~~

On the drive back to Hamburg, Ruth and Karl were able to talk more about the exciting idea of her joining Karl as a camp counselor in the coming weeks. Each summer, he and his friends volunteered at a three-week summer camp. It was designed to give poor children from the city a chance to spend time in the countryside, participate in sports and crafts, and generally just have fun away from home. For Ruth, this would be a new experience, since she had never attended a summer camp as a kid.

When it was time for the camp's planning meeting, Karl introduced Ruth to the other counselors on his team. After hearing stories of her interacting with her five younger siblings, they agreed she was more than qualified to work with them. The counseling team was now finalized with two girls and three guys, and all of them, except Ruth, happened to be over six feet tall.

They all were required to attend two days of training designed to prepare teams of college students across the country to each manage forty 11 to 14-year-olds. Ruth found the other training participants to be wonderful people who believed in giving back to society. Her favorite camp counselor tip was the 'homesick pill,' a sugar pill that could be given with a glass of water to the younger homesick campers; then let the power of suggestion do the rest.

On the first day of camp, some of the kids realized they were taller than one of their counselors, so they jokingly called her Ruthielein. Others called her 'Ruthie from America'. She knew from her own siblings that kids will always try to get away with things, so she and the other female counselor set a no-nonsense tone from the beginning. The children had to get up early, wash, dress, and be ready to eat on time so they could be briefed on the day's activity schedule.

By the second day, the kids had the routine down pat and Ruth had discovered ways to uniquely contribute to the children's camp experience. She decided to hold a 15-minute English lesson each day, and the kids enjoyed repeating simple English phrases to her, and asked her how to say things they wanted to convey. Also, there was an accordion at the camp that Ruth was able to play for sing-a-longs. When the kids wanted a song she didn't know, they'd hum it a few times until she picked up the melody by ear. 'Michael Row the Boat Ashore' was one camp song every German kid could already sing in English.

On July 20, 1969, the camp counselors changed the schedule for the day, so the entire camp could watch an historical event unfold on television, via a live broadcast from America. Neil Armstrong and Buzz Aldrin were about to become the first men to walk on the moon. Hearing conversations in English between Neil Armstrong and the Tranquility Base in Houston, the children kept asking Ruth what they were saying, and she gladly translated.

Then the moment came when Armstrong stepped off of the lunar module and, placing his foot on the moon's surface, announced, "That's one small step for man, one giant leap for mankind." The kids were elated! They were so glad to know Ruthie, an American, someone from the same great country that put a man on the moon! Ruth felt both humbled and in awe—and so very proud to be an American.

~~~~~

The day after Ruth returned home from camp, she received a call from Frau Mensch asking for some help babysitting. Knowing that the Mensch family enjoyed volunteering to provide childcare for neighbors and friends in a pinch, Ruth was happy to oblige.

The child was a beautiful, blond-haired, blue-eyed four-year-old girl who was intelligent, affectionate, and well behaved. Her mother, a single parent, was in the hospital for two weeks with a serious kidney infection. With Karl and his dad both busy working, family friends coming that night for dinner, and out-of-town relatives arriving the next day for a week's visit, Frau Mensch really appreciated Ruth coming over to help.

Ruth enjoyed interacting with the precocious child, who made comments and observations that were both simple and profound at the same time. Being in the loving Mensch home as she played with the little girl, Ruth's mind drifted to Karl's two-year-old daughter. The thought of Sabina not knowing her dad, as well as not knowing her wonderful, loving grandparents and other relatives, was so sad—an incredible loss for everyone. Ruth wanted to talk with Frau Mensch, believing the woman's heart had to be breaking to not be able to hold or even see her only grandchild. But things were too hectic that day, and Ruth never found a good time for such a conversation.

~~~~~

Later that week, it was time to say goodbye to her host family. Ruth thanked Frau Hoffmann, Rolf, and Oma for the kindness, patience, and generosity they had shown her. Ruth gave Oma an extra long hug; and on her way out the door, Oma slipped a small trinket into her hand and squeezed it closed—with a smile.

The last few weeks of Ruth's time overseas were going to be very special. Karl had put in a tremendous amount of time and work preparing for them to take a mini road trip tour of Europe. The route was to start in Hamburg, go south to Bavaria, then on to Austria, with a short visit in Yugoslavia. Next came Italy, Switzerland, Liechtenstein, a brief stop in France, and finally Luxembourg before heading back to Hamburg for the exchange students' flight home.

Ruth loved seeing the famous highlights of the cities they visited and was amazed at the way the size of the mountains increased as they drove from Germany to Austria to Switzerland. They met many interesting travelers as they stayed in youth hostels, dining and playing games together, then splitting up at night into gender-based bunkrooms. And it was only 55 cents per person for an overnight bunk bed and breakfast!

Karl had made arrangements for them to visit a number of friends and family who lived along their trip route. During the Germany segment of the trip, they arrived at the university city of Göttingen and stopped to see the Schneider family, who had formerly lived in the same building as the Mensches. Professor Schneider had tutored Karl in Greek and Latin in exchange for babysitting their daughter, who was now six years old and absolutely loved Karl. While visiting, Karl noticed that a ceiling fixture wasn't working, so he immediately took it apart, fixed the wiring problem, and reinstalled it with sincere thanks from the Schneiders. Frau Schneider said softly to Ruth, "That young man has a great head, a great heart, and great hands!"

Ruth and Karl also stayed one night with Johann and Petra who lived south of Frankfurt in a small apartment. The newlyweds seemed very happy despite having no refrigerator and no stove, using instead a cooler of purchased ice and a single plug-in electric burner for cooking. They were glad to see family from Hamburg.

The first snafu of the trip came in Austria when Karl and Ruth arrived in Vienna, and Ruth realized she had left her cosmetics bag, containing an expensive backup pair of hard contact lenses, at the last hostel in Salzburg. Ruth made what turned out to be a costly long distance call to the Salzburg hostel director convincing him to mail her small bag to Karl's uncle in Graz as soon as possible.

At breakfast the next morning, two guys at the hostel were having car trouble. Karl took a look, and fixed it in 15 minutes. One of the young men asked Ruth if Karl was an engineer. "He's studying to be a teacher," she replied.

While sightseeing later in the day, Ruth had a stomachache, so she slept in the car while Karl toured a technical museum. He then took her back to the hostel where she slept the rest of the day. Karl wanted to see more of Vienna, and ended up sightseeing with the two guys whose car he had fixed earlier.

Ruth was feeling better as they continued

driving through Austria. They visited several of the country's many Catholic churches. Karl said he was baptized a Catholic but had no respect for the hierarchy of the Church. As they passed by collection boxes for the poor, he pointed out all of the ornate gold and marble throughout the building, asserting, "The priests and bishops are hypocrites. The Church should give away its own riches to the poor before expecting the congregation to do so."

Ruth responded, "I see your point, Karl. However, I don't think today's church leaders consider these assets as theirs to pawn. Instead they view the ornateness and majesty of churches and cathedrals as a tribute from generations past, creating an atmosphere to glorify and honor God."

Later, Karl and Ruth made it to Graz, and they were warmly greeted by Karl's aunt and uncle. Within 20 minutes of arriving, Karl noticed that the kitchen sink was clogged and proceeded to fix it, while his aunt and uncle just watched and smiled. Then they informed Ruth that, unfortunately, her contact lenses had not yet arrived in the mail.

The young couple stayed there several days, did laundry, and used it as a base to visit the surrounding area and Yugoslavia. While driving in the city, they experienced another snafu: Karl was stopped by a policeman who gave him a ticket saying he had crossed over a solid yellow line and had to pay a fine on the spot. The couple categorized that traffic ticket fine, along with the charges for Ruth's long distance phone call about the forgotten cosmetics bag, as 'stupidity money' in their trip expense records. Fortunately, her contact lenses arrived before they left Graz for Lienz.

The most harrowing part of their journey came when they drove from Lienz, Austria, through a mountain pass into Italy. Part way up the mountain, it began to rain. The weather worsened as they reached the top and came down the other side. The road was narrow and twisting, visibility was bad, and the windshield wipers had stopped working. With nowhere safe to pull over, Ruth rolled down her window and reached out to manually move the windshield wipers back and forth so Karl could see well enough to drive slowly down the mountain.

They made it safely to the base of the mountain, and stopped at the first restroom they came to, so Ruth could change out of her wet clothes, while Karl found and fixed the wipers' electrical problem. Then they headed to Switzerland, where the roads were better, the mountains were higher, and the plentiful lakes were bluer. The subsequent countries of Liechtenstein, Luxembourg, and part of France seemed plain by comparison.

As Ruth's flight departure day approached, she checked the odometer readings and realized they had traveled more than 4000 km [2400 miles]. The couple discussed sending letters to one another, both writing in their native languages. She was adamant that they both should feel free to go out with other people, at least casually if not romantically. She believed that if their relationship were meant to be long-term, spending time socializing with other people wouldn't damage it while they lived halfway around the world from one another. Karl reluctantly agreed.

"When you miss me," Ruth said, "just look up

at the moon and throw me a kiss, knowing that I will be looking at the same moon six hours later."

Over the coming months, Karl intended to save money, and research travel options to visit Ruth and her family in America, in August of the following year. He winked at Ruth, saying that he also planned to take lessons to improve his English, and advance his ballroom dancing skills.

As they approached the airport, it was only fitting that they heard Peter, Paul, and Mary singing "Leaving on a Jet Plane" on the car radio, just as they had multiple times driving through Europe. They felt like parts of the song had been written just for them:

> 'So kiss me and smile for me,
> Tell me that you'll wait for me,
> Hold me like you'll never let me go.
> 'Cause I'm leaving on a jet plane,
> Don't know when I'll be back again.
> Oh, babe, I hate to go.'

When it was time for Ruth to board the plane, they enjoyed one last long passionate kiss. Then Karl wrapped his long arms around her, and she felt completely lost in his loving embrace.

1. Take pride in your country of origin. It's okay to view your country's achievements as partially your own.

2. Be fully honest about the regrettable stuff in your past as soon as your relationship starts to get serious—the earlier, the better.

3. Know that whenever you have sex, there can be long-term consequences.

4. Begin a long-distance relationship with someone you love knowing it will be difficult. Focusing on the small things you have to look forward to together eases the pain of separation.

Karl in America

August 1970

After more than eleven months of sending letters back and forth across the Atlantic, Ruth and Karl finally were reunited in the Indianapolis airport. He planned to stay with her family for four weeks, and then, when Ruth went back to college, he would spend another three weeks traveling around America alone. He had purchased a special air package for Europeans that allowed him to fly to a number of American cities, within a limited time span, for a very reasonable price.

Ruth gleefully greeted Karl with a hug and a kiss, and then introduced him to her dad who had driven her to the airport. When they arrived at the Starsky family's 5-bedroom 2-bathroom brick house, Ruth's mother was cordial, and her five siblings were curious and talkative during dinner. Karl complimented Mrs. Starsky on the delicious meal, and struggled with his English. Ruth knew he was having difficulty with the fast-paced mealtime conversation, so she reminded everyone to speak slowly.

After dinner, knowing Karl was tired from his flight, Ruth suggested he might want to go to bed early, and he readily agreed. Sleeping arrangements had been modified to give him his own room, and he fell asleep quickly, glad to have made it through the first day. Before Ruth went to bed, she reflected on an agreement she and Karl had made in their recent letters: they promised to decide together by the end of Karl's visit, whether or not to continue their long distance relationship. She prayed, *Heavenly Father, thank you so much for bringing Karl to America safely. Please bless his visit, and make the time Karl and I have together meaningful. Give us the clarity we both need to make a wise decision about our future before he leaves.*

By the end of the first week, Karl felt comfortable with the Starsky family, including all five siblings: Sarah (17), Ellen (14), Kenny (11), Stan (9), and Charlie (4). While the girls were a little leery about this stranger their big sister had brought into their home, the boys loved him, especially when it became obvious that Karl liked sports. He especially enjoyed watching Ruth's dad coach Kenny and Stan's little league baseball team. Stan was a leftie (the only one in the family) and required some individual coaching and a special glove. Her dad was very patient with all the boys on the team, showing them what to do and how to play their positions. Karl commented how inspiring it was to see a father so involved with his children.

Karl made it a point to help out whenever he could, whether it was trimming an overgrown shrub or tree for Ruth's dad, or fixing a broken family clock for her mom. He loved playing games of any kind, and doing jigsaw puzzles with the kids. He often seemed like a big kid himself.

~~~~~

The second week of Karl's visit, some family members decided to spend an afternoon swimming at the local city pool. When Ruth's brothers and Karl came out of the men's locker room, she was stunned to observe him wearing the smallest, tightest white speedo swimsuit she had ever seen. He had never worn anything like that the previous summer in Germany. His attire looked completely out of place among all the baggy trunks that the other men were wearing at the neighborhood pool. Ruth quickly suggested that they all get in the water immediately.

Karl was a skilled swimmer and started doing a few warm-up laps, swiftly gliding from one end of the pool to the other, his long arms moving effortlessly in the water. Then he joined the family playing and socializing in the water.

After a bit, Ruth turned and started talking with her two sisters, when suddenly Sarah said, "Oh, no! Ruth, look! Karl's up on the diving board." Turning around, Ruth and her siblings were horrified. The tight white speedo, now wet and accenting every bulge, looked almost transparent as Karl, using perfect form, dove into the pool.

Ellen commented in dismay, "I'm so embarrassed. We won't be able to show our faces here at the pool for the rest of the summer!"

Then Sarah advised, "Ruth, you better be sure he stays in the pool until we leave, and then have a towel ready, that he can wrap around himself as he gets out."

Ellen remarked with a smirk, "I guess this is one of those 'cultural differences' you were talking about yesterday at dinner."

Ruth later suggested to Karl that they go

shopping for new American swimming trunks that were more like the local style. Somehow she couldn't bring herself to tell Karl how deeply he had embarrassed all of them, and she wondered if last summer she had ever unknowingly done anything 'culturally different,' that had embarrassed Karl or his family.

Suddenly she recalled how she had continued to shave her legs and underarms last summer, like she had always done in America, in spite of the fact that none of the German women shaved. A few of the German female students and even some kids at camp had mentioned to her how weird it was. Ruth thought nothing of it, and continued to shave. Karl had never said anything, but now she wondered if his American girlfriend's odd behavior had embarrassed him.

~~~~~

Ruth's family was always on a tight budget. As a result, they never went on vacation, except to visit their grandparents and aunt out of state. While Karl was a guest, they made an exception, and planned a vacation that included visiting Cedar Point Amusement Park, Niagara Falls, and Washington, D.C. It was a thrill for everyone to experience the majesty of the Falls, the splendor of the nation's capital, and the solemnity of Arlington National Cemetery.

When the family was touring the Capitol Building, Sarah and Ellen observed a man walk past Karl and nod, saying "Guten Tag [Good day]."

Without breaking stride, Karl nodded and responded, "Guten Tag."

"Who was that man, Karl?" Ruth's two sisters asked at once.

"He's my neighbor in Hamburg."

Sarah replied, "You've got to be kidding me. You run into your neighbor from Germany while you are both in a foreign country thousands of miles away from home—what a coincidence! And neither of you even looked surprised!"

Karl shrugged his shoulders. "It's no big deal. I just saw him last month. We're not close friends."

Sarah shook her head. Maybe German men were just reserved when they encountered one another. She was convinced that if two American men ran into each other in Europe, their response would be much more animated and interactive.

~~~~~

On the way home from Washington, D.C., the family stopped in Pennsylvania to visit Ruth's aunt and cousins. Aunt Irene was her mom's jovial sister, who always had plenty of food ready to serve the moment they arrived, including her special homemade pierogies and pizzelles.

Over lunch, Aunt Irene remarked that she had been trying for over a month to get an electrician to add an electrical outlet to her upstairs hallway. There were no outlets in the entire hall, and for years she had to run an extension cord from one of the bedrooms, in order to vacuum the long area. Now, the matter was even more pressing, since she wanted to relocate her sewing machine to the far end of the hall.

Without hesitating, Karl volunteered, "I can do that for you. Show me where you want the outlet, and I will make a trip to the nearest hardware store to get the parts I need."

Ruth wasn't sure that was a good idea. She knew Karl was very handy with engines and electronics, but she wasn't sure about him knocking a hole in her aunt's thick plaster wall, and wiring an American outlet. Before she could express her concern, Aunt Irene said, "I don't want you to go to any trouble—but if you know how to do that kind of work, I would be really grateful." She looked so happy and hopeful.

Pulling Karl aside, Ruth who, like the rest of her family, had never done any home electrical wiring work, asked, "Karl, are you sure about this? Have you done this before? Electricity in America is 110 volts and in Germany it's 230 volts. The outlets and plugs are completely different."

"I am aware of that, but the principle is the same. You cut a hole in the wall and run a wire from an existing outlet to the new one. I can do this for your aunt."

After lunch, Ruth and Karl walked upstairs with her dad and Aunt Irene to check out the location where the outlet was to be installed. Aunt Irene and Karl beamed, while Ruth and her dad looked at one another concerned, not wanting the project to result in damage and/or a future electrical fire.

They next went to the workbench in the basement, and located all the tools needed to cut through the plaster and complete the installation. Then Ruth and Karl headed to the hardware store to purchase the wire, electrical box, outlet, and wall plate needed. There, the helpful hardware clerk gave them detailed instructions, which Ruth paid close attention to as Karl nodded, looking as though this merely confirmed what he already knew. When she asked about the possibility of an electrical fire, the hardware clerk simply replied, "If you do what I told you, and make sure the wires are tightly secured and no bare wires are touching each other, you will have no problems."

Back at the house, they began their project by identifying the circuit that controlled the bedroom outlet they were tapping into, so they could shut off the breaker. Karl worked at a careful steady pace, with Ruth watching closely. She handed him whatever tool he needed, as they huddled on the floor, working back and forth between the bedroom and the hallway. 'Measure twice, cut once' was common wisdom in Germany, as well as in America, and they heeded it well.

Twenty minutes later, the hole in the wall was made, the new electrical box was secured to a stud, and the outlet wiring was complete. Ruth ran back down to the basement to flip the breaker switch. Returning to the second floor, she found a triumphant Karl pointing to a small illuminated lamp from the bedroom, now plugged into the new outlet in the hallway. After more testing, installing both cover plates, and cleaning up, Ruth was pleased that the new outlet looked unassuming—like it had always been there.

Aunt Irene was thrilled! Ruth's parents and siblings were amazed. From that point on, the wall fixture became known as "Karl's Outlet." Ruth was proud of Karl—and she was also very glad that she had learned how to install an electrical outlet.

~~~~~

As Karl's time with the Starskys drew to a close, Ruth saw how everyone had grown to love him. The last week of August, her dad drove the couple from Indiana to Ruth's college in Ohio, which was four hours away. Arrangements had been made for Karl to stay at a boys' dorm on campus for a few days, before Ruth's classes started and Karl had to leave for his three-week tour of America.

During these final days, the couple took a number of long, romantic walks, living each day in the moment. They visualized what their life together would be like if they both lived in America, and alternatively what it would be like if they both lived in Germany.

On their last evening together, they lay in the grass for a long while gazing up at the moon in the night sky. Knowing the time had come for their serious talk, Ruth sat up and gently pulled Karl up to join her.

She held both of his hands, looked up into his beautiful blue eyes and started, "Karl, you know that I love you. You're smart, and funny, and adventuresome, and have taught me so much during the past 16 months. Knowing you has made me a better person. I am so grateful that God brought you into my life."

Ruth paused, looking down briefly before continuing. "The love we've shared will always be a part of me, but I have to listen to my heart. There is something deep inside, holding me back from taking the next step with you."

Karl exhaled as his strong hands went limp. A myriad of thoughts raced through Ruth's mind. *Karl is an amazing person. But he doesn't value some things that are important to me, like a relationship with God and with his daughter. He has an extra year of college to finish after I am done. While both of us say we could be willing to give up our homelands and move away from our families, neither one of us really wants to.*

Ruth continued, "I have prayed long and hard

about us, and I strongly feel God is telling me that you are not the man He intends for me to marry."

Deflated, Karl's hands let go of hers; he lay back on the ground and closed his eyes. After watching him take a few deep breaths, Ruth lay down next to him in the grass, equally wrought with emotion.

Karl finally opened his eyes and turned toward her to speak. "Deep inside, though I don't want to admit it, I know you are right. Although I would like to keep things as they are between us, if we are not meant to marry, then it's best for us to break up today. It's just hard right now for me to believe that I will ever find anyone I love as much as I love my beautiful Ruthielein."

Ruth smiled sweetly, and then added, "I know this will be very hard for both of us, but we must have faith that God will help us find our true soul mates. We will use what we have learned from each other to become a wonderful spouse to the person we each ultimately choose to marry."

Her words were not what Karl hoped to hear, but he nodded as they both gazed up at the moon one last time. Ruth suggested, "I don't think we should write to each other any more, with one exception: whoever gets engaged first should write a letter to tell the other person."

Karl agreed, and walked Ruth back to her dorm. The couple embraced in a long, tearful hug and said their goodbyes. After Karl kissed Ruth tenderly on the forehead, she retreated into the building. Peering out the window, she cried softly as the familiar lanky, dark-haired figure disappeared into the darkness on his way to the boys' dormitory.

1. Know that God sometimes puts people in our lives to love, but not to marry. Listen to the still small voice inside to discern the difference.

2. Realize that once you know you're not going to marry the person you're seriously dating, it is best to end the romantic relationship and move on.

3. Accept that every breakup results in feelings of loss for both individuals, and requires a period of healing.

4. Invite a foreign visitor into your home, and your family will learn a lot.

PART III

> "*Trust in the Lord with all your heart and lean not on your own under-standing. In all your ways acknowledge Him, and He will direct your path.*"
> ~ *Proverbs 3:5-6*

Weihnachtsmarkt

Saturday, December 11, 1999, 7:00 am

Ruth awoke with a start, as the flight at-
tendant announced that Dave and Ruth's plane to
Hamburg would be landing soon. They disembarked early morning on Saturday as scheduled,
exchanged some dollars for Deutschmarks, and
headed for their hotel.

The hotel clerk, Hans, was a tall, blond, good-
looking man in his 30's who spoke English well.
He said the earliest the couple could check in was
1:00 pm, but they could leave their luggage in a
secure room until then. Ruth then asked him the
location of the closest Weihnachtsmarkt, the
German Christmas Market she had always wanted to visit. After Hans marked up a city map as
she requested, she gave him the address of the
Hoffmann flat where she had lived as a student,
and asked him to indicate its location on the map
as well. It had been more than 30 years, but she
still remembered the street and house number.
Hans found it on the city map, and then pulled
out public transportation maps to mark the U-
Bahn [underground train] and S-Bahn [city train] to take
to the Hoffmanns and to Weihnachtsmarkt.

Having flown all night across the Atlantic, Ruth and Dave were both tired, but they stopped for a light breakfast and got a second wind. They headed for the Hoffmann flat first. Recognizing the building and all the nearby shops, Ruth smiled as a flood of memories washed over her—the flower shop where she had bought flowers for her new German family; the little hardware store where she had purchased some pads to fix Oma's wobbly table; and the drug store where she had difficulty explaining to the pharmacist how she was still constipated after a week and a half in this new country and needed some medicine.

When they reached the building where she had lived, unfortunately the front door was locked. Deciding to wait a few minutes, they perked up when a woman approached the building and unlocked the door. Ruth explained that she had lived in the building in 1969 with the Hoffmanns up the stairs on the first floor. (In Germany, the ground floor is level zero and the floor above it is level one.) The woman told them that she had lived in the building for seven years, and there were no Hoffmanns living there during that time. Ruth was disappointed. She knew that Oma was probably deceased, but she had hoped that somehow Frau Hoffmann might still be living in the flat.

Their next stop was Weihnachtsmarkt, and the outdoor market lived up to its reputation as a magical holiday wonderland. The sounds of carols could be heard as the couple strolled through the aisles of intricate Christmas treasures. The scents of wursts and brats, beer and cocoa, and sweets and roasting nuts wafted through the air, mixing with the pine aromas of Christmas trees.

Decorative lights were on, even though it was midday. The couple would have to stop by again after dark some evening, to fully appreciate the artistic illuminated displays.

Dave became engrossed in studying the offerings of a cuckoo clock tent, while Ruth marveled at the variety of ornaments and handmade wooden nutcrackers—soldiers, farmers, kings, and maidens. She was also impressed by the number of manger displays for sale, knowing that church attendance in Germany was at an all-time low. But as someone had once told her, "At Christmastime, everyone is temporarily at least a little bit Christian."

The couple bought some Christmas presents for people still on their gift list. As they finished their stroll, Dave led his wife toward one final vendor he wanted to visit, and then suddenly stopped, half way there.

"Hey, Ruth, look up!" Dave exclaimed, pointing. Gazing upward, Ruth saw a sprig of mistletoe that Dave was holding above their heads.

Ruth smiled, and before she could say a word, Dave kissed her in the middle of the market. "I didn't know if they would have mistletoe in Germany, so I made sure I brought my own sprig from home to make your Christmas Market experience complete," exclaimed Dave.

Ruth thanked him with another longer kiss, recalling a romantic evening exactly 29 years earlier on December 11, 1970, and their very first kiss—which had been under a sprig of mistletoe.

"Okay, now we can head back to the hotel," said Dave.

"Don't you want to go see that clock vendor?" Ruth asked, pointing to a nearby tent.

"Nope, never wanted to," smirked Dave. *The holiday tradition, mastered by the Tanner men, of kissing special women under the mistletoe, was alive and well in Weihnachtsmarkt.*

1. Enjoy the long-forgotten memories that return to you when you visit a place you have not seen in decades.

2. Experience the Christmas season in different countries, if you ever have the chance. The similarities and the differences are both fascinating.

3. Seize every opportunity as a couple to kiss under the mistletoe.

The Helpful Hotel Clerk

Saturday, December 11, 1999, 3:00 pm

Returning to the hotel midafternoon, Ruth and Dave checked into their room and unpacked. Dave mentioned that he needed a few hours to review all of the work materials he had on the expansive trade show that started Monday at the Hannover Messe. Ruth took advantage of her free time to visit the front desk to see if she could find any contact information for Karl.

Heading down the elevator, she thanked God for her husband. Some men would be jealous and uncomfortable if their wife wanted to look up an old boyfriend. Dave was different. Confident in himself and in their marriage, Dave had never been jealous of any of the men that Ruth had worked with, gotten degrees with, or previously dated. One of her former boyfriends had been the photographer for their wedding, and another still exchanged annual Christmas cards with them. Ruth really cared about the people who crossed her path and she always tried to help those who needed her. If God had put it on her heart to find Karl, Dave knew she would do all she could to make it happen.

Happy to find Hans still on duty at the hotel desk, Ruth explained that she was looking for a man named Karl Mensch, who had been a student with her at Universität Hamburg 30 years ago. She hoped he still lived in the city. Hans went out of his way to help her, generating a printout of all the Mensches in the Hamburg phone book file he had on his computer. Because Mensch was a common German surname, there were multiple pages.

The first page of the printout had no first names. The subsequent pages had first names, but she did not see a Karl Mensch listed. She remembered that Karl's brother was named Johann and his dad was named Gustav. There were no listings for Johann, but there was one listing for a Gustav Mensch—it had no phone number listed, only a fax number and an address.

After hearing Ruth's summary of her findings, Hans responded, "Well, there are a dozen Mensches here with no first names listed. Maybe one of them is Karl or someone who knows him. I would be happy to phone each one, explain that I am calling on behalf of a hotel guest who is trying to locate a Karl Mensch, and ask if they have a relative by that name."

Ruth was deeply touched by the hotel clerk's generous offer, and said, "That would be wonderful! Thank you so much."

She returned to her room. About an hour later, Hans called to report that none of the phone numbers he called knew a Karl Mensch. He then said, "Frau Tanner, if you continue to have no luck finding Karl and decide you want to write a fax to Gustav Mensch, I will send it for you. He's probably a long shot, though, since his street address is on the far north end of the city and any-one close to 80 years old usually would not be working and have a fax listed."

"Thank you," Ruth said. "Hans, can you please do me one more favor? This morning I was able to visit the building where I lived in 1969, and discovered the family I lived with no longer resides there. I remember they had an adult son named Rolf Hoffmann who did not live with them. Can you look up his name in the Hamburg phone book and see if you can find a listing?"

Hans took a minute and then returned to the phone. "Yes, Frau Tanner, there is one Rolf Hoffmann living in Hamburg. Here is his phone number."

Ruth told Dave the news, and was hopeful as she dialed Rolf Hoffmann's number from their hotel room phone. A big smile crossed her face as she realized it was the right Rolf.

He confirmed sadly that his mother and grandmother both had passed away. However, he would love to see Ruth again and could meet her and Dave at the hotel for dinner in two hours.

They waited for Rolf in the festive hotel lobby near the huge decorated Christmas tree, and she recognized him as soon as he walked through the front door. He was now about 61 and, other than his graying hair, looked much like he did in 1969.

Sitting down in the restaurant to eat, Ruth barraged Rolf with questions. He explained how his mother had been diagnosed with breast can-cer in 1974, and had died from it in 1976. Oma had been heart-broken, and had stubbornly man-aged to care for her daughter at home up until the end. Rolf described how Oma had refused to ever move out of the flat, even though the steps were too much for her. He had stopped by three days a week while his mother was sick and after she passed, to check on Oma and bring her groceries. Oma had then died from a heart attack in 1978 at the age of 88.

"Oma always liked you," Rolf continued. He pulled out a framed photo he had taken of Frau Hoffmann, Ruth, and Oma sitting on their living room couch in 1969. "She kept this photo on the end table of the living room up until the day she died. She talked about the friendly little American girl who had trouble pronouncing the word 'ich' properly." Ruth was deeply touched that Oma had displayed a photo that included her for so long.

Rolf continued, "She also liked that boy you dated, Karl, ever since he fixed her radio."

Ruth laughed, remembering that day and how happy Oma had been to have her radio working again—it was one of the rare instances Oma actually smiled.

"What about you, Rolf? Did you ever get married?" asked Ruth.

"No, it seemed I was always too busy with work, and Mother, and Oma. After that, I guess I just got set in my ways and never found the right woman. But I am happy and look forward to retiring next year, and moving to someplace warmer than Hamburg."

Dave pulled out a family photo of them with the children, their spouses, and the grandchildren. Ruth talked a little bit about their jobs and their home in Michigan.

When dinner was finished, Ruth reached into her purse and pulled out a small metal figure. "I want you to know that my favorite souvenir from

Hamburg was this little figurine that Oma gave me the last time we saw each other."

Depicting Hamburg's legendary grumpy 'Wasserträger [water carrier]' named Hummel, the base of the figure was inscribed with the famous taunting children's greeting 'Hummel, Hummel,' and the water carrier's equally famous grumpy response, 'Mors, Mors [Kiss my ass]!' To this day in Hamburg, whenever anyone on the street or at a sporting event shouts out, 'Hummel, Hummel,' the automatic expected response is, 'Mors, Mors.'

Rolf laughed and nodded. "Oma always liked the Wasserträger symbol of Hamburg. I think she wanted people to believe that she was just as grumpy as Hummel, but deep inside she had a heart of gold."

On Sunday, Dave and Ruth went sightseeing, including stopping by the university, and then met Dave's colleague, Nate, for dinner. They reviewed the plan for how the trio would get to the trade show in Hannover the next day. Nate had experienced a difficult time getting from the airport to the hotel that morning, so he was very grateful to have Dave's wife along to help navigate.

Monday morning, Ruth emphasized that she was only going to go to Hannover with the men once, so they both needed to pay attention. They would have to navigate on their own the rest of the week. She coached them on what to say to buy the proper tickets, because not being clear could result in inadvertently purchasing tickets for the commuter train to Hannover. This would take much longer than the express train, and consequently shorten their available time at the trade show.

The train ride went smoothly. They walked a short distance and then checked in at the Messe. The three of them spent two hours together just getting an overview of the vendor displays. After lunch, the men left to hear presentations that were being given in English, while Ruth headed for the show's information booth. She hoped that since the Messe trade show was an international event, the people manning the booth might have access to data to help her find Karl.

The man at the information booth listened as she explained her situation. "What you are asking is not directly related to the show, but I think I can help you. I have a database that has the names, addresses, and phone numbers of everyone in Germany, except the unlisted numbers. 'Mensch' is a common German name. If you come back in 30 minutes, I will have a printout of the full list for you. Maybe something on it will help you."

When she returned, she read the printout and saw seven listings for Karl Mensch in various cities throughout Germany. All of them were located hours away in the southern or far eastern part of the country. Ruth felt confident that Karl was not likely to have moved away from northern Germany, especially to the portion of the country that had been the nation of East Germany in 1969. Plus she only had tomorrow—Tuesday—to find him. Wednesday morning she had to be on a plane back to America, so she didn't want to expand her search to include the whole country.

Her eyes were drawn to the familiar fax number for Gustav Mensch that she had seen earlier on Hans's list. She really didn't think the man was Karl's dad, but it seemed that her only option now was to send Gustav a fax, and ask if he knew Karl.

While Dave and Nate were still occupied listening to technical presentations, she drafted a simple fax, first in English, then in German. It read:

To Mr. Gustav Mensch, fax #_____
Dear Mr. Mensch,

My name is Ruth Starsky Tanner. I was a student at the University of Hamburg in 1969. I had a friend, Karl Mensch, who should now be about 55 years old. I would like to speak with him or his parents. Is Karl your son or a relative of yours?

I am in Hamburg only tomorrow (Tuesday). On Wednesday I fly back to America, so please answer yes or no as soon as possible by calling me at the Novotel in room 222 or sending a fax.

Thank you very much.
Ruth Starsky Tanner
Hotel Phone #_____
Hotel Fax #_____

After the trade show, Ruth, Dave, and Nate took the express train back to Hamburg, and went to a restaurant for dinner. When they returned to the hotel, the men went to their rooms and she headed for the registration desk. Again she found Hans, and explained that she wanted to send a fax to the man with the same name as Karl's father, because she had no other leads.

"Hans, I wrote the fax in German and it probably has some grammar errors. Would you please write down the corrections for me as well as the hotel phone and fax numbers?"

He laughed and told her he would be happy to do that. Two minutes later, he handed Ruth her note, marked up with three corrections and the hotel numbers as requested. She sat down in the lobby, rewrote the fax including Gustav's number, and then handed it back to Hans.

"I'll fax this right now, Frau Tanner," he said. "If a return fax comes in within two hours, I will call your room. Otherwise, check with whomever is here at the desk in the morning."

"Can you also mark where Gustav's address is shown on the map?" Ruth asked.

"But, of course," Hans responded. He then promptly put a spot on the map that was on the opposite side of Hamburg from where they were.

Walking back to her room, Ruth said a prayer, *Heavenly Father, you have put such a strong urging on my heart to search for Karl. You even worked out a way for us to stay in Hamburg instead of Hannover. If you really want me to find Karl, please let Gustav be his father or at least, be able to give me a lead.*

1. Don't be afraid to ask people for help when you need it, especially if you are from out of town.

2. Be aware that hotel desk clerks can be excellent resources for local information, and are generally happy to help make your stay more enjoyable and productive.

Gustav

Tuesday, December 14, 1999, 7:00 am

The next morning, Ruth and Dave met Nate for breakfast in the hotel restaurant. While eating food from the sumptuous buffet, including the deliciously memorable croissants, she explained that she was going to spend the day in Hamburg trying to find her former schoolmate. She hoped she would have good news by the time she saw them again at dinner. The men then confidently headed for the train station to go to the Messe, and Ruth went to the front desk to see if there was a fax for her.

Much to her disappointment, no fax had arrived.

Ruth decided she might as well travel across town to find Gustav's home, since his address was her only lead. Speaking with him face to face, she could determine if he was Karl's father, or perhaps knew Karl. She grabbed her purse and her briefcase filled with the research she had gathered, and headed to the train station.

A kind ticket agent explained which trains to take, and how far she would then have to walk to get to the dot on the map that Hans had marked as Gustav's home. Then the agent sold Ruth an all-day pass, allowing travel anywhere in Hamburg and its suburbs. She repeated his instructions, made some notes on the map, and headed for the appropriate platform. Even though the address didn't look familiar, Ruth hoped that when she arrived, she would instantly recognize it as the home where she had visited the Mensch family multiple times in 1969. She liked Karl's parents, and she really hoped to see them again.

Traveling from the south Hamburg station called Hanenbruk to the Hauptbahnhof [main train station], she had to take the underground train U2 north outside of the city to the very end of the line. She left the station, walked straight for a while, and then turned left onto Gustav's street, until she found the specified house number.

As soon as she arrived, Ruth was certain this was not the place where Karl's family had lived 30 years ago. This was a single-family house on a quiet street, not a multi-story building of flats on a busy street. Checking her watch, she noted that it was 9:10 am, took a deep breath, and knocked on the door.

She was surprised when a man around 55 years old answered the door. A big smile came across his face as he said in German, "Ah, you must be the American lady who is looking for Karl Mensch!" He continued, "I didn't see your fax until this morning. I told my wife before she left for work, 'This American lady is looking for someone with our surname. We don't know who he is but maybe we can help her.' I called your hotel this morning and left a message but you must have left already. Please come in and we can talk."

Ruth hesitated. After all, this was a complete stranger. She silently asked God if she should go in, instantly felt at peace, and walked into the house.

Gustav worked out of his home office, which is why he had a fax machine. His house was lovely with beautiful furnishings, a stunning back yard, and a garden.

"Obviously I am not the Gustav Mensch you are looking for. I have only lived in Hamburg for about five years. Before that we lived in Berlin."

He continued, "I could not find any Karl Mensch in the phone book, but I thought perhaps he has an unlisted number. If so, the only way to find out if he lives in the Hamburg area is to go to the government administration office. Everyone who lives in Hamburg has to register there. That is the law."

Every so often, Ruth had to stop Gustav, look up a word she didn't understand in her dictionary, and then nod that she understood, so he could continue.

Gustav resumed speaking, "I will call that government office for you and explain your situation." He dialed the phone and began speaking very fast. She understood him to say, "I have someone here from America who is looking for a Karl Mensch and would like to get some information." He paused, listening to the voice on the other end of the phone. Then he started yelling, "What do you mean we have to write a letter and wait two weeks for a reply? We don't have two weeks. We only have one day to find the man! These rules you have are stupid." He hung up the phone.

Turning to Ruth, Gustav said, "I'm sorry, but

they won't cooperate at all over the phone. Maybe if you go to the city administration office in person, you can talk with them. There may be a form you can fill out to get the information you need."

She asked, "Can you please show me on my map where this office is and how to get there?"

Gustav explained in detail how to get to the government office by taking three separate trains—the U2, the U3, and the S-Bahn—and then walking a long distance.

Ruth thanked Gustav, grateful for the phone call he had made and the new lead that he had given her. She was also grateful for the wonderful Christmas decorations that filled the city, and for a day that was dry, sunny, and not too cold— because she had a lot of walking to do.

Ruth's Journal

1. Be grateful when strangers are kind and hospitable, especially when there is a language challenge.

2. Believe that when God moves you to do a nearly impossible task, He sends people to help you along the way.

Government Offices

Tuesday, December 14, 1999, 10:10 am

Getting on the second train, she sat next to a friendly woman who started talking with her. Ruth was so distracted by the conversation that she missed her station and had to get off the train at the next stop. As she stepped off the U3, intending to take the next train back one station, she looked down the street and saw a long block containing a connected series of five multistory brick buildings. They appeared to have shops on the ground level and four stories of flats above. *These buildings seem familiar; they look a lot like those I remember seeing in the neighborhood where Karl's family lived. But there are probably lots of areas in the city with buildings that look like these.*

After checking her watch, she decided to leave the train station and walk for 10 minutes down the familiar looking street to see if anything specific might lead her to the Mensch flat. The storefronts were decorated for Christmas, and wonderful aromas filled the air as she walked past eateries. It felt like she'd been here before, but she had no idea where the Mensch home might be, if it was even there at all.

Finding a bench, she sat down and pulled out the computer printout containing all the Mensch listings in Germany. She checked to see if any Mensch, regardless of first name, lived on this street. None did, so she stood up and headed back to the station.

Ruth caught the next train back, made the proper connection, got off at Klosterstern, and started asking people for directions. It was a very long walk to get to the right location, and she was especially glad that she had worn comfortable flat walking shoes.

As she entered the government office building, she noticed that it was 11:00 am and there was a line of people waiting. Taking a number from the dispensing machine, she hoped to find someone in the office who spoke English. When her number was called, she faced all the government workers at desks with computers, and loudly asked if anyone spoke English. Those near enough to hear her all shook their heads. She realized that people who worked with foreigners every day—like hotel or airline employees—were likely to speak English, but people working in a city office interacted primarily with the locals, and had no need for foreign language skills.

Ruth did her best speaking with the clerk, explaining her desire to find Karl Mensch, a person who was her friend at Universität Hamburg in 1969. She referred to her dictionary, whenever she didn't understand what the man said.

After checking some records for Karl's name and year of birth, the clerk returned. He reported, "There is no Karl Mensch registered in any of our Hamburg area records, either with or without a published phone number. The only Gustav

Mensch we have in our records is the man you said you already talked with north of the city. Our records are computerized and go back to 1980. If you want to go back further, I can send you to a different government office in another town that has the old records on microfiche."

"Would you please call them for me?" Ruth pleaded. "If they can find a record of him, I will go there."

"Oh, no. There is no way we can do that," replied the clerk, writing down the pertinent information. "You have to go there in person, and ask them directly."

Ruth pointed to her map and asked, "Where is the office I need to go to, where is the nearest train station, and what trains do I take to get there?"

Following the clerk's directions, she took two trains to get to the Harburg—not Hamburg—station. When she got off in Harburg, she asked for directions to the Rathaus [town hall]. It was another long walk. Arriving at 12:15 pm, she realized there was a train station right there, called the Harburg Rathaus station. She could have saved a lot of walking had she known to stay on the train one stop longer.

Ruth retrieved a piece of paper from the last government office where the clerk had written out the exact location and name of the department that could help her. After showing the paper to three different people who directed her through three different buildings, Ruth spotted a sign indicating that the department she was looking for was located on the second floor. Exiting the stairwell around 12:30 pm, Ruth saw a man coming through a red door and approached him for help, pointing to the paper with the name of the department she was seeking. Turning, he pointed to a small sign on the red door and remarked, "That office is only open from 8:00 am until 12:00 pm. It will open again at 3:00 pm for one hour. Come back at 3:00 pm."

Ruth explained that she had to find a certain person today, because she was leaving the country tomorrow. "Please, is there anyone here I can speak with now?"

The sympathetic man told the anxious foreigner to wait there, and he went back through the closed door. Two minutes later he emerged, and waved her in with a big grin. Then, he escorted Ruth through an outer office to an inner office where an older man named Arnold sat at a computer in the corner. She profusely thanked the angelic man, who disappeared as she smiled and then thanked Arnold for agreeing to help her. Like the others, he only spoke German.

As she had done with the clerk in the Hamburg office, Ruth told Arnold all she knew about Karl and his family. After checking some records, he replied, "There is absolutely no Karl Mensch in our computer records. Are you sure he's not dead?"

Ruth had to admit, "Maybe he is. I don't know."

"We have one last place to look," Arnold explained. "Perhaps there is something in the microfiche file in the basement. I will call the lady who is in charge of microfiche." He made a phone call and then they waited.

A few minutes later the microfiche lady called back. Arnold listened and then told Ruth, "She found one German citizen named Karl Mensch—

born in 1944, but not born in Germany. His father's name was Gustav Mensch. Karl left Hamburg in 1975. The forwarding address he registered was in Wintermoor, a very small town south of here that doesn't even show up on most maps."

"That's got to be him!" exclaimed Ruth in an excited voice.

"Let me look up something for you. I happen to have a phone book for Wintermoor," Arnold said, reaching toward the shelf above his desk, which held dozens of phone books of varying thicknesses. The Wintermoor book was very thin. "Let me see if I can find someone named Mensch living in Wintermoor at this address."

After a pause, he continued, "Ah, I found a listing for Mensch, but it is not Karl. It is Brigitta Mensch. It is probably his widow."

Trying to stay positive, Ruth responded, "Or perhaps he's divorced."

Arnold replied doubtfully, "Maybe, but I think he is probably dead."

"If Brigitta is his widow and she is in Wintermoor," Ruth stated firmly, "I still want to go there. If he has passed away, then I want to know how he died, and as many details as possible about the life he lived after 1970."

Arnold wrote down Brigitta Mensch's name, address and phone number. Ruth considered calling her, but decided not to. It was hard enough to speak German in person. Speaking on the phone was more difficult, lacking the benefit of facial expressions and hand gestures to help communicate thoughts. Ruth decided she would go to Wintermoor and just walk up to Brigitta's door.

"To get to Wintermoor, you will have to go north to the Hauptbahnhof in Hamburg and then take an intercity train to Wintermoor," he explained.

She was overjoyed with the new information that Arnold and the microfiche lady had provided. Ruth gratefully said, "Vielen Dank für alles [Thanks a lot for everything]." As she left the office, she reflected on two new things she had learned:

First, in 1944, during World War II, Karl was born outside of Germany. He never mentioned that to me. Maybe his parents fled the country during that time...or, since I know Karl has relatives in Austria, maybe he was born there and moved to Germany with his parents after the war.

Second, in 1975, Karl left Hamburg to live in the small town of Wintermoor. This was five years after I last spoke with him. And there is a woman with his last name still living at that address 24 years later. Could it be his wife? His ex-wife? His widow? Or his daughter?

Arnold had surmised that Karl was dead, but deep inside, Ruth did not believe that was the case. She felt confident that much would be revealed in Wintermoor. After all, it was almost Christmas, a perfect time for a miracle.

Ruth's Journal

1. Don't underestimate the power of persistence. It frequently is the one thing that makes the difference between failure and success.

2. Realize that often in a foreign country, when you don't speak the language well, face-to-face communication is most effective.

Wintermoor

Tuesday, December 14, 1999, 1:30 pm

Ruth walked to the train station and took the S3 back to the Hamburg Hauptbahnhof. She bought a round-trip intercity ticket to Wintermoor, as Arnold had instructed her, knowing that the city was too far away for her day pass to be valid. Since it was now 2:15 pm and the intercity train would leave at 3:15 pm, she had an hour to eat lunch and use a pay phone to call the hotel.

Hans answered the hotel phone. She asked him to leave the following message for her husband in room 222:

> *Dave,*
> *I got a good lead and I'm going to the town of Wintermoor to continue looking for Karl. I will not be back for dinner. See you later tonight.*
>
> *Love,*
> *Ruth*

"Wintermoor?" questioned Hans. "I've never heard of it."

"Well," said Ruth, "I'm hoping it's a town where I will find out what happened to Karl."

"Good luck, Frau Tanner!" replied Hans.

"Thanks," Ruth exclaimed. "And Hans, by the way, God bless you for speaking English! I needed that right now."

At 3:15 pm Ruth got on the train and was shocked when after 25 minutes, the intercity train pulled into the Harburg station, which is where she had departed from after talking with Arnold a few hours earlier. Speaking with a young woman in the next seat, Ruth asked, "Is this the same Harburg train station where I can get the S3 back to the Hamburg Hauptbahnhof?"

The young woman responded, "Oh, yes, you can get the S3 from this station." Disappointed, Ruth realized she had lost several hours of search time by traveling from Harburg to the main train station in Hamburg and back again because Arnold had told her to do so.

The train pulled away from the Harburg station, continuing south. As the two strangers resumed chatting, the woman asked about Ruth's final destination. "Wintermoor," was her reply.

"This train doesn't go to Wintermoor. Let me see your ticket."

Now in a panic, Ruth pulled out her ticket and saw that the word 'Buchholtz' was written on the ticket between 'Hamburg' and 'Wintermoor'. The lady looked at her ticket and said, "You have to change trains at Buchholtz. And that's the station we are approaching now!"

Luckily Ruth was able to get off the train. She had only two minutes to catch the next train that would take her to Wintermoor. The man in Hamburg who sold her the ticket had said nothing about changing trains. Of course, she should have been smart enough to study the ticket while she was waiting for an hour before departure. She was so grateful for the lady on the train, and thought of her as a 'travel angel.' *If not for her, I probably would have stayed on the train until the conductor came to check my ticket and who knows how much more time I would have lost!*

Upon arriving in Wintermoor, Ruth was surprised. Every other train station she had ever been to had one or more buildings, a large platform, some parking nearby, and a paved street out front. The Wintermoor stop was nothing more than a small wooden deck next to the train tracks and surrounded by a field. Ruth felt like she was literally 'in the middle of nowhere.' Even worse, since it was mid-December, the sun had already set and darkness was closing in.

With the little daylight that was remaining, she found a path through the field that seemed to be heading toward a building in the distance. After less than a minute's walk, the path intersected a nine-foot wide gravel lane that she hadn't noticed earlier. Fortunately right at that moment, a man was walking down the lane toward her. She breathed a sigh of relief, hoping he was another 'travel angel,' and asked for directions to the street she had listed for Brigitta Mensch.

"Follow this road and take the first left turn. Walk until you pass a Gasthaus [country inn] and then turn left again. Hopefully the house you want is not too far down the road because it's a long street."

"Danke," said Ruth, grateful that he knew the way. It was a pleasant stroll through the tiny, charming town that was all decorated for Christmas. Ruth walked past a Gasthaus and then turned left. Fortunately, between the Christmas lights and a first quarter moon, she was able to see well enough to make her way down the road.

Brigitta's street had an interesting mix of small farms and residential properties. Another 20 minutes of walking elapsed before Ruth arrived at the house she was looking for. No interior lights were on. Checking her watch, she realized it was nearly 5:00 pm. She knocked on the door once, then twice. No one answered.

She noticed what looked like a business sign on the front lawn, but she couldn't tell what was written on it. Spotting a woman near the road several houses down, Ruth walked over to her and asked if she knew the Mensch family. The woman replied curtly, "No, I don't know or talk with any of my neighbors."

Ruth then headed in the other direction down the street to Brigitta Mensch's next-door neighbor's house. There she encountered a woman about her own age, putting a bag of trash into a garbage can near a lamppost by the street. Ruth asked her if she knew the Mensch family.

"I know Brigitta," the woman replied cautiously.

"Do you know Karl?" Ruth asked, hoping to find out if he was dead or alive. She pulled out a picture of Karl that she had in her purse.

Holding the 30-year-old photo under the light of the lamppost, the woman nodded and replied, "Karl hasn't lived here in a long time. They are divorced." *That neighbor's nod of recognition is the best thing that has happened to me all day! Arnold was wrong—again.*

"Were there any children?" Ruth pressed.

"No, no children." She started to look uncomfortable, like she regretted telling a stranger as much as she had. "I don't know anything else. I just talk occasionally to Brigitta. She is very busy. She works a lot and is not home much. I can't tell you anything else.

Ruth said, "Danke," and walked away. She happily thought, *Karl's alive! Maybe Brigitta knows his current phone number and address. I really need to speak with her.*

She figured she had two choices: either sit on the front porch and hope that Brigitta would come home soon, or walk 20 minutes back to the Gasthaus, and figure out what to do next. She decided on the second option—primarily because she needed to use a restroom.

1. Understand that sometimes people un-intentionally give you wrong information. It's usually best to 'trust but verify.'

2. Know that when you are on a journey, comfortable walking shoes are always better than fashionable alternatives.

3. Appreciate the 'travel angels' you encounter when you are in a new place. Be prepared to serve as one yourself when you see a visitor struggling or confused.

The Gasthaus

Tuesday, December 14, 1999, 5:25 pm

Ruth walked back to the Gasthaus she had passed earlier. Christmas carols were playing and there was a festive atmosphere inside. She went into the restroom, and before leaving, she stared at herself in the mirror. She wished she could look like the cute, thin, young girl she was in 1969, but that wasn't going to happen. At least when she had left the hotel this morning, her makeup had been freshly applied and her hair nicely combed. Now she looked like a tired, slightly disheveled, overweight grandma. Doing her best to refresh her face and hair, Ruth realized that at least her smile and her eyes were still the same. She had started the day wanting to look nice in case she found Karl. Now, after miles of walking and taking countless trains, she didn't care how she looked—she just wanted to find him.

After asking the Gasthaus employee wearing a Santa hat behind the bar if she could use his phone, Ruth pulled out the number for Brigitta that Arnold had given her. She wasn't sure if Brigitta would be home yet, but she had to give it a try, because she had no desire to walk all the way back to her house for nothing. She was surprised when a woman answered the phone.

Ruth began, "Hello. My name is Ruth Starsky Tanner. I went to Universität Hamburg with Karl Mensch in 1969. Do you know him?"

The woman replied, "Yes, I was married to him, but we are divorced now. Is this Ruthie from America?"

"Yes, it is." She was stunned. *Even though I always went by the name Ruth, 'Ruthie from America' was the name Karl used in 1969 whenever he introduced me. Why would his ex-wife be so quick to know or remember that?*

Brigitta replied, "Just a minute. Let me find Karl's phone number. He doesn't live in Wintermoor. He has remarried and lives in another town about twenty-five kilometers [15 miles] away."

After writing down Karl's phone number, Ruth thanked Brigitta and said, "I had hoped to meet you. I've been curious."

"I have been curious, too," Brigitta replied. "Where are you now?"

"I'm here at the Ecke Gasthaus in Wintermoor."

"I'll be right there," Brigitta replied.

"OK." Ruth thought it would be good to perhaps have something to drink and talk for a few minutes to the woman Karl had married. She sounded very nice.

While waiting for Brigitta, Ruth dialed Karl's phone number. A man answered right away.

"Hello. This is Ruth Starsky Tanner. Are you Karl Mensch?"

"Yes, but who are *you*?" Karl sounded confused.

Remembering what Brigitta had called her,

she responded, "Ruthie from America."

"Ruthie Starsky?"

"Yes." She found it interesting that Brigitta, a woman she had never met, recognized her faster than Karl.

"Where are you?"

"In Wintermoor," she replied. "I am in Germany for one day and thought that if you weren't busy, we could get together."

"I'll be right there. Where should I meet you?"

"Don't come right away. I need a few minutes. Meet me at the Ecke Gasthaus at 6:15."

Karl replied, "I will be there at 6:15."

Just as she hung up the phone, Brigitta arrived. Ruth asked if she wanted to join her for something to drink.

"Oh, no. I don't want to meet with you here. People in this town talk too much. I want to take you back to my house."

"Please speak slowly," Ruth requested. "My German is not the best."

Brigitta was an interesting person—serious, thin, and average in appearance, with shoulder length light brown and gray hair. She explained that she and Karl had married in 1972, right after they both graduated from the university. They had stayed married until 1993—a total of 21 years. They had no children and she was very glad they got divorced—in fact, she thought they should have divorced much sooner, because they were both happier not married to each other.

After cordially offering Ruth something to drink, Brigitta explained that she ran a small business from her house, was often away meeting with clients, and did all the paperwork at home. Then she provided a tour of the house that she and Karl designed and had built in 1975. Ruth noticed that the only Christmas decoration was a small wreath on the door. Brigitta said, "Karl told me about you, and you are in the family pictures of Karl's brother's wedding in 1969." Ruth had never seen those photos.

Ruth told Brigitta about her marriage to Dave in 1971, about their son in Indiana and daughter in Boston, their two young grandsons, the granddaughter that was on the way, their jobs, and their home in Michigan.

Brigitta knew that Karl was coming to the Gasthaus at 6:15 and she wanted to get Ruth back ahead of schedule so she didn't run into him. They arrived five minutes early and Brigitta nervously said, "Oh, no. Karl's here already! That's his car right there in the parking lot. We've only seen each other once since we divorced six years ago."

Karl got out of his car and saw Ruth chatting with Brigitta. As he walked toward the women, his puzzled expression seemed to convey, *Why are you talking with my ex-wife?*

Ruth got out of Brigitta's car and, sensing Karl's surprise and disapproval, she spoke brightly, loud enough for Brigitta to hear, "Karl, it is so good to see you. I am so grateful to Brigitta for giving me your phone number. Because of her help, I am able to see you tonight!"

Karl nodded a curt acknowledgement toward Brigitta, but didn't smile. A definite coldness passed between them. As soon as Ruth closed the car door, Brigitta sped away and Karl politely opened the passenger door of his car to welcome 'Ruthie from America'.

1. Remember that tracking down someone whom you haven't seen in a long time can be intimidating. It's only natural to be hesitant, because you don't know what kind of reception you will receive.

2. Push through your fear and discomfort and accept whatever outcome is the result, especially when your heart is moving you to take action.

3. Be cordial and kind when meeting the spouse or ex-spouse of someone you dated a long time ago. It is likely that they are as curious about you, as you are about them.

PART IV

> *"For it is not you who speak,
> but the Spirit of your Father
> speaking through you."*
> *~ Matthew 10:20*

Dinner for Three

Tuesday, December 14, 1999, 6:15 pm

In the car, Ruth was trying to control the surprise she felt as she gazed at Karl. He looked nothing like the dark-haired, clean-shaven student she knew 30 years ago. Still tall and thin with bright blue eyes, this man before her had snow white hair, a hefty white beard that concealed most of his face, and looked older than her father—more like Santa Claus than her former boyfriend. He had absolutely no wrinkles, and she told herself that if he shaved his beard and dyed his hair, he would probably look more like a 55-year old. He had gained maybe 15 pounds but carried it well on his 6'2" frame and did not look overweight. To her, the white hair was okay, but she had never liked beards.

As Karl drove, their conversation was a bit awkward at first. Ruth answered in a simple manner all of his preliminary questions—'Why are you in Germany? When do you have to leave? How did you find me?' She tried to get accustomed to the sound of his voice again, because he just didn't seem the same to her—more like a stranger than someone she had once known very well. It didn't help that while he was driving, she couldn't see his eyes, one of the few things about him that remained unchanged.

Ruth told him she had been back to Germany a few times for business, but never anywhere near Hamburg. As she talked, she used the word 'Sie,' which is the polite formal form of the word 'you' used in business or with strangers.

Suddenly an irritated Karl muttered, "If you don't start saying 'du,' I won't answer any more of your questions." 'Du' was the informal familiar form of the word 'you' that Germans used for family and friends.

Ruth replied, "You must understand that the few times I have spoken German in the past 30 years were for business, and I had to use 'Sie.' I will try to remember to use 'du,' but if I forget and you don't like it, we can just start talking in English."

Karl laughed and shook his head. He didn't want to do that even though in 1969 his English had been as good as her German. When he laughed, she saw, for the first time, a hint of the old Karl from her youth.

As they arrived at his home, she asked, "Is your wife going to be here?" Ruth didn't want to surprise Karl's wife with her presence and possibly create an issue.

"No problem. She was at a tennis lesson when I left the house, so I wrote her a note explaining I was picking you up. I don't know if she is home now or not. Don't worry. It will be fine. Come on in."

Karl's wife, Frieda, was not home yet, and his note to her lay unread on the kitchen counter. Even though it was dark out, Karl wanted to show

Ruth around the outside of the house, turning on some outdoor lights and pointing out the interesting features of the back yard. There was a large pond surrounded by small structures—a general workshop and storage building, a beekeeper's box for collecting honey, a chicken coop with four chickens, and a woodworking shop.

"I have a good life here with Frieda," Karl elaborated. "My first wife was insecure and very jealous. Every time she saw me talk with any other woman, she would get angry and stay mad for several days. Life with her was very difficult." Ruth knew that Karl was a naturally outgoing and friendly person, who was always talking with people he encountered. His first wife was probably angry a lot.

As they walked, he continued, "Frieda is self-confident and not jealous. Our life together is much more peaceful and we both like sports." He paused. "Let's go in the house and get something to drink."

They entered the house through the back door just as Frieda was entering the house through the front door. Karl immediately introduced the two women and from her expression, Ruth had the feeling that Frieda recognized her name. Then Frieda responded, "Oh, yes. You're Ruthie from the family wedding pictures Johann has on display at his house." Both wives had now mentioned these photos and Ruth had never gotten to see them.

As they sat down at the kitchen table to talk, Ruth watched Frieda's polite neutral expression. Earlier Karl had mentioned that his wife was 45—five years younger than Ruth, and ten years younger than Karl. Frieda was about 5'9", of average build, had brown eyes and brown hair cut one inch below her ears similar to Ruth's, was somewhat attractive, and was very toned and athletic—quite the opposite of Ruth, who had always been the last person chosen when any teams had been formed in gym class.

Frieda explained that she had worked in a bank for a number of years and then had become a teacher. Karl worked as a teacher of science and 'sport' just as he had planned. Ruth recalled how much Karl loved children and how well he had interacted with her younger siblings. Frieda and Karl had no children, but both loved their students and enjoyed nurturing them and watching them grow up.

The two-story home was very modern with a 16-foot high ceiling in the living room. It was festively decorated for Christmas, including a very tall Christmas tree in the center of the rear wall. The back of the house was mostly comprised of large glass windows, with a view of the pond and back yard. Frieda had built the 2300 square foot house and then, in 1993, she and Karl had started dating after his divorce. When they married in 1995, Karl had moved in. They planned to start building a new and smaller one-story home together in a few years.

Ruth told Karl and Frieda about the two houses she and Dave designed and had built. She then showed them a Tanner family picture, which included their two children and spouses, and their two young grandsons.

"Our first granddaughter will be born in a few months," commented Ruth.

"You look far too young to be an Oma!" Karl exclaimed. Ruth was pleased by his comment.

When Frieda asked if it had been difficult to find Karl, Ruth said it had been a real adventure. She then proceeded to walk Frieda and Karl through the highlights of her search. When she mentioned how she could not find a listing for Karl Mensch in the phone lists for Hamburg and northern Germany, Frieda explained, "That's because our phone number is listed under my name, not Karl's."

Ruth continued talking about the fax, the visit to the unrelated but helpful Gustav Mensch, the government office in Hamburg, the government office in Harburg, the critical clue in the old microfiche file, the long trip to Wintermoor, and the help provided by Brigitta. As she recounted her day's adventures, Ruth realized how everything had worked out for the best. Even the hours she lost inefficiently traveling from Harburg to Hamburg, and then back through Harburg to Wintermoor, had served a purpose in getting her to Brigitta's house, close to the time when Brigitta returned home for the day. Karl and Frieda marveled at her story and at her perseverance.

"I couldn't give up," Ruth explained. "I only had one day to find you."

After they chatted for a while, Karl walked over to a nearby bookcase and pulled out a photo album from his 1970 trip to America, when he had spent a month staying with Ruth's family in Indiana, and then three weeks traveling around the country on his own. She was surprised that he had such an album so readily accessible with no advanced notice. She, on the other hand, had searched for several hours through old boxes stored in her basement just to find one photo of Karl before she left with Dave on this trip.

Karl remarked how much he had enjoyed spending time with Ruth's parents and five younger siblings. His presence plus special family trips to Cedar Point, Niagara Falls, and Washington, D.C., had made it a memorable month for the Starsky family as well. He had pictures of it all, and he also had photos of Ruth's dad coaching little league baseball with two of her brothers. Karl talked about how impressed he had been by her dad's coaching and her mom's cooking—both parents had spent a lot of time with their children. Ruth was really touched and told Karl that she had never seen a photo of her dad coaching baseball. He promptly pulled out one of several similar coaching photos and gave it to her to keep.

She was almost embarrassed that Karl was reviewing this well-organized book of their time together with both her and his wife. Ruth glanced over at Frieda, to see if she was feeling uncomfortable about their extended reminiscing. Frieda seemed okay, and her expression remained neutral and polite, even though she was probably a bit bored. In the back of the album was a large envelope containing the letters Ruth had sent during the year they were apart. When they had exchanged letters with each other, he had always written in German and she had always written in English.

Pulling out the last letter in the envelope, Karl said, "This is the final letter you wrote to me on March 15, 1971, just six and a half months after we broke up. In it you wrote that you got engaged to a man you had only known for three and a half months. You spoke so highly of him and explained why you decided to marry him. I am going to make a copy of this letter and I want you to give that copy to your husband as a gift from me."

Frieda then turned to Ruth and asked, "How did you meet your husband?"

Ruth smiled as she reminisced, pausing periodically to recall the German words needed to tell them the story of how she met Dave:

"Our paths first crossed at the university in Ohio in mid-November of 1970. It was 9:30 pm and I had just finished a strenuous two-hour kick line dancing practice. I was wearing old sweat pants, looked quite disheveled, was badly in need of a shower, and didn't want to see anyone I knew. However, I had to make a fast stop at the library before going home to my dorm to study for a test I had the next morning.

"Walking into the library reference room, I set my belongings down on a study table, and went to search the nearby shelves. I returned to the table to write down the key information I needed from the reference books, and then left as soon as possible to go back to my dorm.

"Two days later, my phone rang. The caller said, 'Hi, my name is Dave Tanner. You don't know me, but I was sitting across from you in the library reference room on Tuesday night. I noticed that your electromechanics textbook was the same one I used when I was studying engineering at the University of Wisconsin a few years ago.'

"I responded, 'My major is physics, not engineering' and then I asked suspiciously, 'How exactly did you get my phone number, Dave?'

"Dave replied, 'While you were searching for a book on the reference shelf, I reached over and opened your electromechanics textbook and saw your name written on the top of the first page. Yesterday, I called the university operator, asked for the phone number of a student named Ruth Starsky, and she gave it to me.'

"I hadn't noticed him in the library, but now I was intrigued for three reasons: first, many guys are intimidated by girls who have technical majors, but Dave obviously wasn't; second, he had seen me looking my absolute worst and was still interested; and third, I thought his strategy for obtaining my phone number showed ingenuity and confidence. I liked the sound of his voice and decided to keep talking with him for a while.

"At the end of the phone call, we agreed to meet for two hours the following Sunday to eat pizza, which ended up being our first date."

Frieda remarked, "That's quite a story! Speaking of going out to eat, Karl and I would like to take you to a nearby restaurant for dinner."

Looking at her watch, Ruth saw that it was 7:45 pm. Dave was probably back in the hotel room, so now would be a good time to call him.

Frieda showed her to a phone, and when she called the hotel, Dave answered on the first ring. "Good timing. I had dinner with Nate and just got back to the room five minutes ago. I got your phone message. When I read it, I asked the hotel clerk where Wintermoor was, and he said he had never heard of it before. So I got a little concerned. Did you find Karl?"

"Yes, I did," Ruth replied. "It's a long and complicated story that I will tell you later. I wanted you to know I'm okay. Right now I am going out to eat with Karl and his wife, and then I'll take the train from Wintermoor back to Hamburg. It will probably be another three or four hours before I get back to the hotel."

Dave responded, "Ruth, I'm pretty tired because Nate and I did a lot of walking through the trade show today, so I may be in bed when you get here. Be sure to take a taxi from the train station to the hotel. I don't want you walking around Hamburg alone so late at night."

"Dave, just so you know, Hamburg is a very safe city, much safer than most cities in America. But, to make you happy, I will take a taxi from the train station to the hotel."

As Frieda, Karl, and Ruth walked to a nearby restaurant, Karl started talking about his parents. His dad was about to turn 80. His folks lived in southern Spain nine months out of the year, only returning to Germany for the summer. They loved Spain because the temperature was moderate and it was much less expensive than Germany. Ruth was reminded of all the 'snowbirds' she knew—Michigan retirees who left for Florida or Arizona once the weather turned cold. But they didn't have to speak a different language while enjoying the warm weather during the winter months.

Ruth mentioned that she couldn't remember his parents' address, but she named the particular train stop where the area had looked familiar.

He said, "You were right. Mom and Dad used to live just down the street from that station."

Karl, Frieda, and Ruth entered the restaurant, which was festively decorated for the season, and the owner showed them to a quiet table in the far corner. Karl took out a camera and asked the owner to take a picture of them. After the photo, Karl explained, "This is my friend, Ruthie from America. I have not seen her since we studied at the University 30 years ago. Isn't it wonderful that she found me after all this time! We came here to eat because we want to be sure she gets a fine dinner." The owner flashed a big smile, winked at Karl, and went to get the menus.

The three diners started to discuss the price of gasoline and how long it took each of them to commute to work. It took Karl and Frieda 20 minutes to drive to work. They couldn't believe that Ruth and Dave both had jobs that were 80 kilometers [48 miles] from home. The fuel costs had to be terrible.

Ruth replied, "Not really. Both of us are managers and have company cars. The company pays for the fuel, insurance, maintenance, and all the other costs associated with the cars we drive." Then she pulled out her company business card and handed it to Karl. He looked very surprised when he read her title 'Technology Planning Manager.' "It's not fun driving in heavy traffic nearly an hour each way to work, but we like our home and we enjoy our jobs, so the long commutes are worth it to us. We listen to a lot of books on tape while driving, since we have little time to read printed books."

Ruth then talked about turning 50 soon, and how she had decided to celebrate by searching for a few people who had made a big difference in her life. Her high school physics teacher was one, and Karl was another. She explained how Karl not only had helped her improve her German speaking ability, but also had been kind in including her in activities with his family and friends, while she was so far from her own home. Karl had also sparked in her a desire to get a teacher's license to supplement her physics degree.

Turning to Karl, she continued, "Dating you for four months in Germany and one month in America made me a better person. You taught me a new way to solve problems, by simply looking around and creatively using whatever resources were available—like the time when you used my nylon scarf to replace a broken belt on your car's engine. In the time we spent together, something wouldn't work, someone's vehicle would break down, or a delay would occur. You might get frustrated for a moment, but you always thought of an action that could be taken. To this day, I try to be like you, whenever I face a difficulty. Believing that every problem has a solution, if we are open to creative alternatives, has helped me throughout my life. Of course, I still pray to God for help first," Ruth teased Karl with a small smile.

Karl laughed at this, suddenly remembering their religious discussions many years before. He knew God was a big part of her life and though he had attended church with her family in Indiana a few times, he still was not one to pray regularly.

With dinner over, they walked back to the house. Frieda commented about how she herself could not speak any English and was amazed at how well Ruth spoke German. Frieda then shared how her brother had married a woman from New York. They had been living in Frankfurt for the past five years, and his wife still couldn't speak much German. Throughout the evening, Ruth had stopped their conversation several times when she didn't understand something Karl or Frieda had said, and she either checked in her dictionary or asked them to say it again using different words. Overall, their evening's conversation had gone very well.

Now it was time for her to leave.

As she checked to be sure she had both her briefcase and her purse, she noticed Frieda across the room talking quietly to Karl, and then Karl nodding his head.

Walking over to Ruth, he explained, "Frieda thinks instead of driving you to the Wintermoor train station, I should drive you all the way back to the hotel—and I agree."

Ruth protested, saying, "It's too far, you have to work tomorrow, and I already paid for a return trip train ticket from Wintermoor to Hamburg."

Karl insisted and she finally agreed. She thanked Frieda for her hospitality and Frieda gave her a big warm hug. "I'm glad you came," Frieda said, smiling.

"I'm glad I came, too," Ruth replied.

1. Don't be surprised if talking with someone you have not seen for years or decades seems a bit awkward at first. Things will improve as the conversation progresses.

2. Consider that if you are included in the family photos of someone you are dating—especially wedding pictures—those photos will be around for a long time, even if you aren't.

3. Be gracious when your spouse brings home an unexpected guest. It could be an interesting evening.

4. Reflect on this: "And we know that in all things God works for the good of those who love him, who have been called according to his purpose." (Romans 8:28).

Driving to the Hotel

Tuesday, December 14, 1999, 9:50 pm

There was not much traffic on the country roads as Karl and Ruth drove back to the hotel. As they continued to talk, Ruth remarked, "What surprises me the most is that you had no children with either Brigitta or Frieda."

"Yes, me too," responded Karl. "I love children and wanted a lot of them just like your father had. I thought your large family was wonderful. With Brigitta, we kept putting it off, first to work and get financially stable after graduating from the university, then to build the house, then to decorate the house. I finally realized that deep inside Brigitta really didn't want to have children, at least not with me. With Frieda, well, she thought it was too risky once she turned 40. She loves the children at school, but she likes to come home and not have to take care of them."

"Do you ever hear from Sabina?" asked Ruth. It was the first time she had brought up Karl's daughter born out of wedlock since he told her about it on the beach in 1969. Now Ruth realized that Sabina was probably going to be the only child he would ever have.

Karl responded that he never sees his daughter and has no idea how she's doing, although he heard that she had gotten married a few years ago; her mother had never married. Ruth asked if he was an Opa [grandfather] yet, and Karl replied, "I have no idea, but I doubt it."

"If you don't mind me asking, why have you remained so distant from your daughter? When she does have children, don't you want them to know their Opa?" asked Ruth.

Karl explained that for years he never had any contact with Sabina or her mother. Then a situation came up in 1993, right after he and Brigitta had divorced. Germany had passed a law stating that an illegitimate child over 18 years of age could claim a birthright and request an advanced inheritance from her father. The court would decide how much money the one-time payment should be. By accepting that court-determined amount, the child would give up any future claims, including money from her father's estate when he died.

Karl had been devastated when he received the court order and summons. He contacted Sabina who was then nearly 26, and told her that because of his recent divorce, it was a very bad time for him financially. He asked her to wait a few months before proceeding, but unfortunately she said no. Then he asked why she was doing this. He didn't know if she really needed the money, if she was vindictive because he had never paid any child support, or if she felt entitled to a lump sum payment simply because it was the law. She never answered him.

A short time later, after Karl had finished paying Sabina the court-ordered settlement amount, the law had been repealed. Karl was still angry about it and had not spoken to his daughter since. Ruth was secretly glad to hear that Sabina had received the money.

After hearing his story, Ruth felt certain that God wanted her to speak with Karl about the importance of forgiveness. Karl had always been a kind and loving man—unless you did something to hurt or anger him. Then, in his mind, you no longer existed—you were erased or crossed off of the list of people in his life. There was absolutely no forgiveness. Sabina's mom was off the list. Sabina was off the list. Brigitta was off the list. It suddenly occurred to Ruth that perhaps she, too, had been off the list.

"Karl, does not speaking with your daughter make you happy?"

Karl answered, "She hurt me so badly that I can't even stand thinking about her, let alone speaking with her."

Ruth replied, "You know, they say the only people who can hurt us deeply are the ones we love the most. Is it possible that you really love Sabina even though she has not been a part of your life?"

He said nothing.

She continued, "Have you ever thought about how hurt *she* must feel having a father who rejected her from the day she was born, especially since her mom never married, and she never had a stepfather or other father figure in her life?"

Karl shook his head. "Sabina and her mother were part of my youth, a big mistake I made. I didn't want to complicate my life with Brigitta, and now Frieda, by having contact with a child from my past. It seemed best to stay away."

"I'm not suggesting that you immediately contact Sabina and reconcile," Ruth clarified. "That's something you would need to think about and discuss with Frieda. But I do think you should at least consider forgiving her in your own heart. This unforgiveness you have been carrying for so long is a heavy and unnecessary burden that is a barrier to you experiencing real joy, peace, and happiness."

They were now getting close to the hotel, and the intensity of their conversation changed as snow began to fall and their attention shifted to navigating the city streets. Once the hotel was in sight, Ruth felt inspired to continue, "Karl, God sent me to Germany, and helped me to find you, against all odds. I think He sent me to tell you that as your heavenly Father, He loves you infinitely and wants you to be happy. That can't happen until you remove all the unforgiveness in your heart by forgiving Sabina, her mother, Brigitta, and anyone else who hurt you. Eventually you may even decide to ask Sabina to forgive *you* for not being there for her while she was growing up."

Ruth knew that what a person thinks affects what he says; and what a person says affects what he does. It was her hope that Karl would take the first step and change his thinking. The rest would follow naturally in time.

Karl was silent as he pulled into the hotel parking lot. Turning off the key, he looked directly at Ruth and said, "You have given me a lot to think about."

She smiled warmly and took a deep breath. A feeling of peace came over her as she realized that although she still had many questions for

Karl, she had used her final time with him to convey the message that God had intended for her to deliver.

Karl got out of the car, and came around to open her door. When Ruth stepped out into the gently falling snow, he closed the car door, looked down at her with his charming smile, and gave her a big hug. Despite their bulky winter coats, his long arms wrapped completely around her. She had forgotten how tall he was and how his hug would envelope her and she could get completely lost in it. She felt young and petite—for just an instant, she felt like Ruthielein again.

"I'm glad you never stopped looking until you found me," he said appreciatively.

"I am, too. Before you leave, please come into the hotel lobby for just a minute. I'd like to introduce you to some of the hotel staff who helped me to find you. Also I want to call Dave and see if he wants to come down to meet you." She looked at her watch. It was 10:40 pm.

As they entered the lobby, sparkling with its large Christmas tree and holiday decorations, Hans looked up from the reception desk and saw Ruth with a large grin on her face, accompanied by a stranger. He enthusiastically asked, "Frau Tanner, did you find Karl?"

"I did and I wanted you to meet him, so you could know how the work you did for me paid off. I think finding Karl in one day was a Christmas miracle and you were part of it."

After the introductions, Hans pointed to a woman who had stopped her work at the other end of the reception desk to peer over at them. "I'm sure my colleague wants to meet you both. Everyone here has been talking about the American woman who was trying to find the German man she knew in college 30 years ago. The staff will be glad to hear there was a happy ending."

After another round of introductions and some jovial laughing, Ruth said, "Hans, may I use your phone to call my room to see if Dave is still awake?"

He dialed room 222 and handed her the telephone. A sleepy-sounding Dave answered after four rings, "Hello."

"Hi Dave, Karl ended up driving me to the hotel, so we're both downstairs in the lobby now. Would you like to come down to meet him real quick before he leaves?"

Dave had gone to bed before 10:00 pm, completely exhausted from his day at the trade show. He told her he had no interest in coming down now to meet Karl. Ruth realized that this was a matter of curiosity versus discomfort. If your curiosity is higher than your discomfort (as it was for both Brigitta and her) then you do it. If your curiosity level is lower, then you don't.

"Okay. I'll say goodbye to Karl and be up in a minute."

Karl walked with Ruth over to the elevator as 'Silent Night' played softly in the background. He pulled out a card and said, "Here's my email in case you need to contact me."

His American friend didn't take the card, and instead explained, "Sorry, but I'd rather not. We both are married to people who deserve our complete attention." She smiled warmly. "I think the next time we communicate will be in heaven."

Ruth stepped into the elevator, turned around, and hit the button for her floor. Then she said in English with a smile, looking directly into his bright blue eyes, "Be happy, Karl. Always know that you are loved. Merry Christmas!"

As the elevator doors closed, Karl smiled, nodded, and replied in German, "Du, auch, Ruth. Fröhliche Weihnachten [You, too, Ruth. Merry Christmas]!"

When Ruth reached room 222, she quietly went into the bathroom, cleaned up, changed into her night gown, and then slipped into bed. Cuddling next to Dave, she whispered, "I know you want to get back to sleep, so I'll tell you all about my adventures tomorrow. I just want you to know that I am so-o-o glad I'm married to you."

Dave rolled over and kissed her warmly.

Ruth's Journal

1. Listen closely to what other people tell you, and to what God puts on your heart to say in reply. He may be using you to convey His wisdom or help someone at just the right moment.

2. Consider how holding on to unforgiveness hurts you more than it hurts the one who injured you. Once you make the decision to forgive, let go of the hurt and let it flow out of you. Only then can you really experience peace and joy.

3. Believe that miracles happen every day, not just at Christmastime.

The Letter

Wednesday, December 15, 1999, 6:30 am

As Ruth packed for her trip home, she began telling Dave about her journey to find Karl. Expectantly she pulled out the old letter that Karl had copied for Dave, and gave it to him to read.

March 15, 1971

Dear Karl,

I hope all is well with you and your family. When we last spoke, we agreed that the first one of us to get engaged should write the other a letter. This is the letter about my engagement.

In mid-November, I met a student named Dave Tanner. He is 26 years old, works six days a week as an engineer for a large company, and is taking classes four nights a week to get a Masters degree in Business Administration. His great-grandparents came to America from Germany.

Despite knowing each other for only a short time, we found we have much in common, are strongly attracted to one another, and love each other very much.

Besides being a hard worker, Dave is smart, funny, confident, persevering, handsome, and friendly. He is never jealous, does not hold a grudge, and is quick to forgive when someone hurts him. He likes sports, and has the same views that I do on religion and sex. Dave has good judgment, and gets along with my family, as I get along with his. He wants to have children and supports me in whatever career choice I want for my life.

The only thing I wish Dave would improve is his dancing!

A month ago, I prayed long and hard, and God gave me a peace that Dave is the person He has planned for me to spend the rest of my life with. When Dave proposed a few weeks later, I said yes. I am graduating at the end of April and we plan to get married in early August.

I wish you much happiness, and hope that you find a special person to share your love and life with. You are a fine man who deserves the very best.

Love,
Ruth

Dave looked up at Ruth after he finished reading. "Well, that's quite a letter. It had to have been hard for Karl to receive something like this." Ruth nodded slowly in agreement.

Glancing back at Ruth's words of admiration, he asked with a smirk, "Now that you and I have been married for 28 years, do you think you'd still write about me in the same way?"

"Absolutely—except my list of desired improvements might be a little longer," she responded playfully. They both laughed as Dave pulled her close for a kiss.

The couple once again joined Nate at breakfast. Although Ruth had already shared some details of the search for Karl with Dave, Nate pressed her for even more. "I can't believe you actually found the guy," said Nate. "You are the most persistent woman I've ever met."

Dave chimed in, "Nate, you have no idea. My wife often quotes Winston Churchill who helped the Allies win World War II with his motto, 'Never, never, never, never give up!'"

*1. Consider agreeing to send a future letter
to someone you recently broke up with, to
let him or her know when you eventually
become engaged. It helps to bring about a
more complete closure and eliminates any
lingering unrealistic hopes that may exist.*

*2. Pray earnestly for God's wisdom when
choosing your lifelong spouse. Go forward
only if you have the peace that comes from
making a critical decision that is aligned
with His will.*

*3. Remind yourself often: "Love never
gives up, never loses faith, is always hopeful and endures through every circum-
stance." (1 Corinthians 13:7).*

Christmas Travel Plans

Saturday, December 18, 1999

With Dave and Ruth both home from their Germany trip, they were now focused on the details of their upcoming Christmas travels. The third Tanner grandchild was due in a few months, so their son, Clark, had asked for his parents' help to create a children's play area in his basement. The young family could really use the extra finished living space. Dave and Ruth decided to spend their remaining vacation days in Indianapolis, tacking four days on to the beginning of their usual Christmas trip.

"Hey, Ruth, you know Clark said that they want to take us out for a nice dinner on your birthday on Wednesday," said Dave.

"We'll probably be busy working on the basement. I'd be happy with just ordering pizza that night," suggested Ruth. "I don't want to lose any critical work time due to my birthday."

"Fifty years deserves to be celebrated with more than just pizza, Ruth! We're going to stop working and go out for a nice dinner that night. End of discussion," insisted Dave.

Ruth appreciated his gesture even though she was more excited about the basement project and

Christmas than celebrating her birthday.

Ruth and Dave began making a packing list for their trip and setting aside the items on it that were ready to go. They had to think about extra materials needed for the project work at Clark's in addition to luggage, food and presents they needed for the busy holiday trip. This year, like every year, their Christmas travels would involve visiting both sides of the family, driving from Michigan to Indiana to see Ruth's family on Christmas Eve, and from Indiana to Wisconsin to see Dave's family on Christmas Day.

Every Christmas Eve, Ruth's mom and dad, affectionately called Nana and Papa, would host the Polish vigil known as Wigilia. With the six siblings plus their families in attendance, the party was always large, joyous, boisterous and the highlight of the year. Nana would cook a fabulous traditional fish feast including shrimp cocktail, scallops, white fish, and shrimp scampi; family members would assist with side dishes and desserts. Papa prayed a special blessing, and then everyone would exchange kisses and pieces of a thin wafer called Opłatek; this was a Polish Christmas tradition emphasizing family unity, as symbolized by the Holy Family images embossed on the wafers.

After dinner, Ruth's son-in-law would take group photographs of the family and then the Christmas program would begin. All of the children, starting with the youngest and proceeding to the oldest, would perform a song, poem, skit, dance, or other entertainment to the enthusiastic applause of the family members. Then Ruth's siblings and their spouses would take turns reading the Christmas story in segments, separated by the singing of Christmas carols related to each portion of the story, ending with Nana and Ruth's favorite, 'Silent Night'.

The Christmas music was provided by the family's polka band—Ruth's three brothers playing the accordion, saxophone, and trumpet. To accompany them, Papa would play a novelty instrument called a Boombass percussion stick. Mounted on a modified pogo stick—that he would push to the ground for every downbeat— were a tambourine, cowbell, block of wood, and cymbals—one of which he would strike with a drumstick on each upbeat. When the readings and singing were finished, Ruth's sister, Ellen, would bring out the 'Baby Jesus Birthday Cake,' a large cherry-glaze-filled sheet cake dessert, topped with a porcelain Baby Jesus in a manger and a single candle. The children would surround the cake with everyone singing 'Happy Birthday' to Jesus, and the youngest child always had the privilege of blowing out the candle.

All of the children would then each be given one 'family gift' to open, purchased by their parents with money provided by their aunts and uncles. Nana and Papa also would present an envelope containing a cash gift to each member of the family. Dessert and coffee would then be served with the family polka band playing again, and everyone would spend the next hour dancing with one another in Nana and Papa's large living room. Papa, even with his advancing age, was the best dancer in the family.

Dave was an only child, so Christmas Day visits with his parents in Wisconsin were much quieter, and very special in a different way. After an eight-hour car ride from Indiana, family members would be greeted by Dave's dad, who loved maneuvering the ladies to stop under the mistletoe for a kiss. Veggies and a homemade soy sauce dip were served along with pre-dinner drinks while Christmas carols played on Pa's record player. Ma was always busy in her immaculate kitchen putting last minute touches on the Christmas Day dinner.

For dessert, the Tanner family's traditional Christmas cookies would be served. Ma had used the same recipes every year since Dave was a child, and would make one kind each day the week before Christmas and then store them on her kitchen counter in large, hand-labeled tins. No one—especially Dave and Pa—was allowed to touch the cookies until after Christmas dinner. Everyone saved room for the special treats— especially the chocolate chip and frosted animal cookies.

After dinner, everyone would move to the living room where presents were stacked in front of each seated family member, ready to be opened slowly, one at a time, going around in a continuous circle. Appreciative comments were always made and the giver was sincerely thanked. Each person would receive a large package of M&M's from Santa, and every year Dave was gifted the same 'extra' present from Mrs. Santa—new underwear—just like when he was a kid. Relaxing and playing games, like backgammon and Scrabble, while nibbling on candy and Chex mix out of Ma's vintage glass candy dishes and jars completed the celebration.

Ruth really loved thinking about their upcoming Christmas—every part of it. She snuck downstairs to wrap Dave's gift on the ping-pong table where they had their wrapping station set up. She couldn't wait to see the look on his face when he opened the present—the cuckoo clock she had secretly purchased when he was in the restroom at the Weihnachtsmarkt.

1. Visit the elders on both sides of the family during the holiday season, even if it entails a lot of travel. You, your children, and your elders will make priceless memories together.

2. Incorporate as many holiday traditions as possible from both sides of the family, in addition to starting new ones.

3. Recognize that Christmas traditions are memorable, not just because of the beautiful or delicious results, but, more importantly, because of the special people who share in the experience.

Ruth's Birthday

Monday, December 20, 1999, 11:00 am

With a car packed full of presents and tools, Ruth and Dave arrived at their son's house in Indiana. Clark was standing outside to greet them with the garage door open. "Marie ran an errand with the boys, and she accidentally locked me out. Since I don't have a house key with me, we will have to wait until she gets home to go inside."

Ruth responded, "Maybe not. Do you have any doors that don't have a deadbolt?"

"Yes, the door between the garage and the kitchen," said Clark, pointing inside the garage.

She went back to their car and took out a can of peanuts she and Dave had been snacking from during their car trip. Popping off the plastic lid, she used Dave's pocket Swiss army knife to cut off the rim of the lid. Then she flexed the plastic, aligned it with the center of the doorknob and slid it between the narrow face of the door and the frame. She moved it around until she felt the tongue retract and the door opened.

Handing the modified peanut can lid to their son, Ruth laughed and said, "Here, Clark. You can keep this in the garage as a spare key!"

Clark commented, "You know, Mom, I tried using my credit card to do the same thing before you got here, and it didn't work."

She smiled and replied, "Many credit cards are too stiff. Peanut can lids are strong and can flex without breaking, so they perform a lot better. We're just lucky I had one in the car—since we really need to use your restroom after our long car trip!"

The three of them went inside and soon started working in the basement. Ruth installed the boxes and rough wiring for the basement electrical outlets, while Clark and Dave followed behind her installing drywall. Then she followed behind them and finished wiring the outlets while they worked on the drywall seams.

They worked for two days straight and were well into Wednesday when Clark said, "Mom, don't forget that Marie, the boys, and I are taking you and Dad out to dinner for your birthday tonight. Everyone has to be in the car by 5:30 pm so we can make it on time for our reservation."

As 5:00 approached, Ruth wanted to keep going until she got to a break point, so while the others left to get ready, she continued working. At 5:15, she heard an anxious voice call out, "Ruth!" as her clean, well-dressed husband appeared at the top of the stairs. She had to stop now or she'd make them all late. Ruth put down her tools, ran up the steps, hopped in the shower, threw on a pants suit, and figured she could comb her hair and put on some makeup in the car. Her mom's familiar words came back to her, "If you're wearing a smile, people won't notice anything else." They all left in Clark's van at 5:30, right on schedule.

At 6:00 pm the van pulled up to a beautiful, fancy country club. Ruth was concerned because this place was way too expensive for Clark's teacher salary. She was escorted upstairs to a private party room when a loud chorus of "Surprise!" rang through the room. Ruth was totally flabbergasted. Her entire family was there—even Aunt Irene and Ruth's cousin, who rarely traveled from their hometown in Pennsylvania. Like most people born in late December, Ruth's birthday had always been just an afterthought at Christmas. An actual birthday party just for her, two days before the family Christmas Eve celebration, was unbelievable.

Dave had scheduled and paid for the party. Their daughter Kate had done the planning, the invitations, the menu selection, the flowers, the favors, and the decorating—all from Boston. She had thought of everything—even videos in an adjacent room in case the young children became restless.

The food was delicious, and there was a small program including a slideshow that Kate's husband prepared, using photo contributions from the family, chronicling Ruth's past 50 years. Family members shared both serious and funny stories along with words of heartfelt appreciation. Everyone enjoyed the trip down memory lane.

At the end of the program, her brother Kenny brought out his accordion, and passed out copies of a song sheet to everyone. Then he and his wife led the family members in singing special lyrics they had written as a tribute to Ruth, using the music from Dean Martin's classic song, 'That's Amore.'

Call Ruth Tanner (That's Amore)

When your car is broke down,
And you're stuck in Motown,
Call Ruth Tanner.
When your toilet is jammed
And you're needing a hand,
Call Ruth Tanner.

She's a plumber, electrician, mechanic,
engineer, and musician.
She's a leader, a scholar, a teacher,
a wife, and grandmother.

When your life's in despair,
'Cause you have no career,
Call Ruth Tanner.
She will give you advice,
And she won't charge a price
For your call.

She went to Hamburg to learn,
She rose high at her firm,
She knows Jesus.
She is thoughtful and kind,
A great blessing you'll find,
In Ruth Tanner.

HAPPY 50TH BIRTHDAY, RUTH!!!
WE LOVE YOU!!!!

Ruth sat there with tears in her eyes, unable to speak, as the last remnants of the blues associated with turning fifty completely melted away. She didn't realize until now that she had made such a difference in the lives of her family members over the years. Her heart was so grateful that God had blessed her with a wonderful family and a life of contribution, opportunity, and adventure.

As the family applauded with joy, her mother came forward with a small gift. "Happy Birthday, Ruth!" she exclaimed with a sly smile and a hug. As Ruth opened the gift, her eyes widened and her jaw dropped. Inside the old-fashioned box, Grandma Sophie's pearls shined as light from the overhead chandelier reflected on them. "Grandma Sophie wanted you, as her oldest granddaughter, to have these," said Nana.

Ruth lowered her head and pulled her hair forward so Dave could attach the necklace clasp. As Kenny began playing 'Zosia'—also known as 'Sophie's Polka'—her favorite dance partner whisked her away. Dave watched as Papa and his daughter reunited with delight on the dance floor, knowing it was the perfect start to whatever God had in store for Ruth's next decade.

1. Convey gratitude to people who organize a surprise party for you. It's not easy!

2. Remember that expressing sincere words of appreciation is one of the most precious, memorable presents you can give.

3. Observe that every decade of life has its own adventures and blessings.

4. Spend less time thinking about aging as a diminishing, and more time viewing it as an accumulation.

EPILOGUE

Two and a half years later, Ruth received an unusual email at work. The body of the email contained no words—only a single photo. In the picture stood Karl, holding a beautiful, laughing, blond-haired girl, probably about three years old, who was caressing his thick white beard with her two small hands. Both Karl and the little girl were gazing adoringly and lovingly into each other's eyes.

The email subject line contained one word:
Opa

Read another book written by Pat Schuch:

_Driving in the Middle Lane__:_
Business and Life Lessons
From the Auto Industry

For book discussion questions
and more about the author, visit:

integraresources.org

Made in the USA
Columbia, SC
21 August 2020